THE TRAITOR'S BRAND

A MYSTERY BY HUGH RUSSEL

Cover design: Hugh Russel

Hugh Russel's portrait is by Denni Russel Photography

Photos from public domain Illustrations are collage compositions with Photoshop graphic filters

Published: February 5th, 2022

Library and Archives Canada

Paperback ISBN: 978-1-7777946-2-0

eBook ISBN: 978-1-7777946-3-7

Published by:

Negative Space Publishing

For my Friends Tony Hillman and Tony Reynolds
'And thanks for all the fish.'

And a note to my daughter who said I never mentioned her in
by dedications. BTW it's not true.
Hello Nicole! ☺

IF

"If you can talk with crowds and keep your virtue,
 Or walk with kings—nor lose the common touch;
 If neither foes nor loving friends can hurt you;
 If all men count with you, but none too much;
 If you can fill the unforgiving minute
 With sixty seconds' worth of distance run—
 Yours is the Earth and everything that's in it,
And—which is more—you'll be a Man, my son!"

Rudyard Kipling

Index

Index

Part ~ 1

Bartholomew Bigelow
Butterworth
Brother~Betrothed~Bastard
1882~1913

CHAPTER ~ 1

THE LIEUTENANT COLONEL

His had become a peaceful life, simply using the skills he had developed while serving with the British army in India and South Africa. However, on this rather pleasant day, that idyllic simplicity he had grown to appreciate, was about to be ripped from him, and send him headlong into an investigation of death and tragedy that, for a time, would even transcend a world at war.

Lt. Col.
James Wilson Horn

Lieutenant Colonel James Wilson Horn had retired from the army, a life he loved and though his service to the British Empire and his King would never truly end he was depressed and plagued by frightful dreams. After a miserable year or so of doing nothing, he decided to put his skills to use and pass the time productively by solving small mysteries. There were too few to keep him busy, yet it was a satisfying enough occupation to contemplate. He had a close friend who, for the second time became his investigative partner.

It was Major Anthony Hillman, with whom he tested and refined those special skills over many years in the army.

During the recent war in South Africa, they had travelled under cover in enemy territory, gathering intelligence. It seemed appropriate that in peace time, they should continue to work together in the same way.

Both bachelors, James and Anthony had their own flats in a house James

Major Anthony Hillman

owned in London. Sergeant George Findley served with them in the field and was fatally wounded in a skirmish against a handful of Boer guerrillas. As he lay dying, he asked James and Anthony if they would look in on his wife Sylvia from time to time, just to see that she was doing alright. He was a good friend and a thoroughly decent man, so of course they promised they would.

To keep their promise James brought her up to London and employed her to run his house and look after them. It was an arrangement which satisfied all involved. Save for the fact that Mrs. Findley was rather talkative, and forever listening at keyholes.

Their practice of private and independent investigation had several high-profile successes. For that reason, since 1909 James and Anthony had become loosely connected, through the joint initiative of the Admiralty and the War Office, to what is now called the Secret Intelligence Service (SIS).

During those times when there was nothing of national importance to investigate, and those times seemed to last forever, they worked on their own to pursue civilian investigations and pleasurable pastimes.

James, a decent artist, had engaged in a hobby, for want of a better word, which allowed him to rest his brain from the stress of city living. His objective, while remaining in the city, was to be in peaceful surroundings and out of doors. He chose to wander the parks and cemeteries of London in search of interesting things to note and draw.

On this pleasant day in late June, he was ambling through the Brompton Cemetery, armed with a sketchbook, a box of pencils and other materials he might need if a subject appealed to him.

His method of finding that particular thing that spoke to him was to scan beyond the ubiquitous crosses and slabs of stone faded by years of weather, and to seek out the unusual. Those objects which most people would never see, works of art which had employed imagination, personality and, even in some instances, whimsy. With drawing materials in hand, he would study and sketch them. If he found one of particular beauty he would record it in fine detail. As well, he even transcribed the odd epitaph that amused him, and some were very odd indeed.

What caught his eye on this day was a stone that stood out because it was so new, bright and polished amongst the faded tablets. This 'new boy' had two distinct points of interest. The first was the rather cryptic and rude inscription: Brother, Betrothed, Bastard.

The second was a design, chiselled with the same care as the inscription, but on the right edge of the stone and as a veteran of the South African War, James found its message very disturbing. When referring to a man, as this design most certainly was, there could only be one possibility as far as James could see. The man who lay rotting beneath that stone had been branded as a traitor.

✳✳✳✳

The Origin of the Brand

Though the war against the Boers had ended twelve years since, James could never forget that mark. Having noted the name of the deceased and the insulting epitaph, he sketched the mark then began his journey home.

The Brand

It was while he was walking to the exit that a second idea struck him. This inscription and the added mark encapsulated a mystery that could provide him with some measure of entertainment. With a little more spring in his step, he set off in search of the caretaker's office.

The man he spoke with would not readily be engaged in conversation, and limited his comments to a few grunts, a nod or two, and the telephone number of the management authority. That was enough to get him started, so he hired a cab and headed for home.

Immediately following his return to Number 5 Warwick Square he called the agency and had a brief conversation with a clerk in the cemetery's office. It seemed, he thought, that the staff of the Cemetery Management, had been chosen because of their utter lack of conversational skill. Though the exchange was far from entertaining, the information he received served to provide a touch of drama to the mystery.

There was apparently, no family involvement in the purchase of the plot, the burial, or the headstone. The transactions were conducted through the offices of a solicitor representing the deceased, by a second anonymous client. "Isn't that a rather odd bit of business?" James asked.

"It's got nothing to do with me, sir. I simply assigns the plots and keeps the records. You want to know more, then I suggest you go ask the solicitor."

So, that is precisely what James planned to do and telephoned to make an appointment. The firm was located in the Flat-Iron building on the West Strand, and the solicitor was Mr. Fenton J. Hardcastle, QC, of the firm Young, Thurborn, Davidson, and Hardcastle. He agreed to see him the next morning at 10:00. James arrived for his appointment precisely at 10:00 am.

It never ceased to amaze him, how the smells of the city permeated everything. Humanity's ability to replace the sweet smells of the open country was a never ending source of regret. Yet that slight breeze that followed him as he entered the front room was further tainted by the smell of the perfume introduced to ameliorate it. The unwashed bodies of the gaggle of clerks, and stale tobacco smoke went unnoticed by the people within, but were a momentary shock to the system for James. All could be banished, he thought, by the introduction of an open window or two.

His welcome was equally bracing with the less than cordial greeting from a Dickensian horror known as Mr. Hickory Stoat, the firm's clerk. With a nasal voice that matched his twig-like stature he said, "I feel that I must remind you, sir, that Mr. Hardcastle is extremely busy, and his time is precious to the firm. See that you don't waste it."

Narrowing his gaze, James removed his glasses and looked down on Mr. Stoat with a raised eyebrow, and with as much calm as he could muster, replied, "An appointment was scheduled for ten o'clock this morning, was it not?"

He sneered, "Apparently so."

That rudeness did not sit well with James. His temper rose quickly when confronted by such behaviour and his voice dropped low and menacing as a lion's does when meeting a rival. "Apparently so?"

The fear response was as intended, and realizing that he overstepped, Stoat recalibrated his tone and posture to explain himself, "Colonel Horn. If you will permit me, I meant only that…"

"Let me stop you before you waste anymore of my time. Show me to Mr. Hardcastle's chambers at once."

"Of course, sir. "This way." As quickly as his attitude had improved, the old Stoat returned. When they arrived at the office door he pushed it open and barked, "Mr. Hardcastle."

From somewhere buried behind the stacks of files and books there lurked the man James had come to see. "Yes, Stoat, what is it?"

"Your ten o'clock is here," he announced, then scurried away.

"So soon?" The disembodied voice grumbled. The sound had come from a dark place near the far window. "Good heavens. Well, show him in if you must."

James surveyed the cluttered chamber. "It would seem that I am already in, Mr. Hardcastle."

"Oh, what? Uh, well that's… uh fine." There was a rustling of papers and frustrated breathing. "Where did I leave my… oh, they're right here. Splendid."

The office had every appearance of a work in progress, and from that James began to form an opinion of the man that was quite different than the one who welcomed him. The whitewashed walls were bare save for the framed diplomas from the colleges where he absorbed his profession. Simple but sturdy wooden shelves lined two walls and were filled with precedent setting cases and law journals.

His cluttered desk was piled so high with documents marked read and to be read that he was all but invisible behind it all.

He was overworked to be sure and seemed to be truly uninterested in the usual trappings of his profession, but keenly interested in the law. Before laying his eyes on him, James felt an instant sympathy for the man.

He stood, combed back his thinning hair with his bony fingers and smiled, allowing James the opportunity to see the man for the first time since entering the office. "Colonel Horn, is it?"

"Yes, a pleasure Mr. Hardcastle, good morning." Reaching over the precarious mess James performed a perfunctory handshake. "Is it? I often wonder," he said, glancing at the door with quiet humour. "The way people avoid me around here one might think I am diseased. Now, to the question that brought you here. Have a seat... if you can find one."

"Thank you," He lighted on the chair that Hardcastle apparently had not seen in years. Then parting the stack of papers as if it was the Red Sea. "Aha, there you are," he said, as he sat, almost disappearing again.

"Hello again," James uttered with a smile he couldn't resist. "I am given to understand that your office arranged for the burial of Mr. Bartholomew Bigelow Butterworth."

"Did we?" asked the aging solicitor, as if it was something crucial that he may have missed. "I don't seem to recall... Uh... Mmmm... Uh... Oh... wait just a... a... Butterworth, Bartholomew...Patience, patience 'B' for Butterworth." James had become quite used to dealing with his fellow Englishmen's eccentricities, and this one seemed rather likeable. "Oh yes... Tut-tut-tut, silly of me. It should be in this book... uh... no." He set aside the large ledger, turning his attention to a small notebook which his fingers happened to find within the cavernous jumble on his desk.

"Yes... this seems to show some promise... uh-hah, this is it." Thumbing through it from back to front, he asked, "What year would that have been?"

James smiled. "Nineteen-hundred-and-thirteen."

"Uh hah... thirteen... thirteen... oh yes, finally, here we are. Butterworth, Bartholomew Bigelow." He recited the name as if calling from the attendance at school. "Billing? No, that is not what we want. Uhhh... I'm terribly sorry, I... am usually... much more..." He was about to give up when his eyes brightened, and he actually smiled. "Oh, at last. How simply marvellous. Yes, 'B' for Butterworth, it is coming back to me now. A strange situation, that one, as I recall. I believe there was no family left in England to take care of his estate, so the client left the details to his friend, uh Mr. ... oh yes, wishes to remain anonymous." He laughed briefly.

"Almost gave it away, didn't I?" Looking over the rims of his spectacles. "He took it upon himself to act as the executor for the estate. It was quite a small undertaking as Mr. Butterworth had little left to his name. He saw to all the final arrangements through our good offices and paid the outstanding costs."

"A fairly routine business, was it?"

"Not a bit of it," he sputtered quickly, and took off his glasses. "Not the usual sort of thing at all. I was given very specific instruction as to the style of stone to select, and what was to be inscribed upon it. There was to be no reference to any religion and, as I recall, there was some sort of profanity in the text of the engraving. I could look it up for you ..."

"There is no need, I have seen the stone."

"Have you now? Well, thank heavens for that."

"There was a symbol engraved on the side of the tablet," James said, leading the man to the second point of his visit.

"Uh Hah. What extraordinary business, not the sort of thing one puts on a grave marker."

"How was it described to you?"

"I can do better than describe it. The man gave me a drawing which I passed along to the stone mason. Here, see for yourself." He held up the page. "Very odd. I have no idea at all as to what it represented. I suspect that, as with the text, there was something rude and unsavoury about it. I suspect some boys will never grow up. None of my business, of course. I merely execute the wishes of the client."

"Of course."

He continued, "A lot of fuss about nothing I thought." And then stopped, eyeing James closely. He was a shrewd old man and curious too. "But since it seems to interest you, perhaps I was mistaken?"

He was possibly hoping for something to make this trip down memory lane more interesting. James let his question hang in the air for a moment before he answered. "To be perfectly truthful, it was simply a matter of personal curiosity."

"Uh hah, I see."

"And now that I have uncovered all there is to it, I can dismiss the matter and move on."

"Mumm, humm, well I suppose it's for the best. One shouldn't dwell too long on the past." James could see how disappointed he was, and he let the solicitor stew in it for a while, hoping it might allow the client's name to bubble up. But no joy there. "I am glad to have been of some assistance."

"You have, and I thank you for it. Oh..." He paused as he stood, "There was just one other thing."

"Yes?" he responded eagerly.

"You mentioned that there were no relatives."

"Living in England, I believe I said."

"Of course. Are you, by any chance, aware of any family members living or dead who may have been abroad at the time?"

"Uh…" he fought with that question for a few seconds, weighing the pros and con of giving out too much information. "Again, my accursed memory fails me."

"If it is too much trouble then by all means…"

"Hang on for a moment. You young people are always in such a hurry." Amused by that remark, James watched him as he opened the journal again and found his place. "Oh yes, here it is. Yes, there was a sister, a Miss Jennifer Butterworth. I have the address here. Sorry I should have mentioned that before." He paused.

"A problem?"

"Oh, well dear me, I'd forgotten about this entirely."

"You had forgotten what?"

"It was the strangest thing."

"What was?"

"The client demanded that I inform his sister of his death. He dictated the contents of the letter to me. I was to say that there were outstanding affairs of business which required her attention, and that she should return to London."

"And was that so strange?"

"In a way, yes. You see, to my knowledge, he had taken care of every last detail. I reminded him of that, but he remained adamant. He said they had a few very personal matters to discuss and thought that it would be more persuasive coming from the solicitor." Handing James a blue tissue copy of a letter, "That is what I wrote, there. I regretted that the letter contained not so much as a modicum of sympathy for the grieving woman. But then the client wants what the client wants. It didn't seem to matter though, as I have not heard back from either the sister or the client."

James scanned the letter noting that it had been written on January 11, 1913. He handed it back.

"Thank you. Uh... you said you had the address."

"Oh yes, number 10 Rue Rousseau, apartment number 210, Geneva, Switzerland. Did you get that?"

James wrote it down quickly. "I did, many thanks. You have been most helpful Mr. Hardcastle, I am much obliged."

"Perhaps you could return the favour."

"Perhaps, what do you require?"

"You might tell me why you wanted this information."

"Oh." He looked thoughtful as if he might have said, 'Well, it's simple enough I suppose. It's just some amateur detective work. It has become a hobby of mine, to observe the unusual objects found in London cemeteries. That particular bit of text caught my attention first, and then I noticed the odd symbol on the side.'

Instead, he kept it simple. "There was nothing special really, it simply piqued my curiosity."

"Did it now?" Having immediately lost interest, he said, "Then, I hope your curiosity has been satisfied."

"It has, and again many thanks."

"You are welcome, and a good day to you, sir."

"And a good day to you."

As he left the office James ran into the clerk, who had been perched by the door like a vulture, waiting for payment. "There is a fee for the solicitor's time," he said.

"Fair enough Mr. Stoat. Will a pound cover it?"

"It will indeed," he said, testing the pull-strength of the note James handed him.

Clear of the building on the steps above the pavement he felt relieved to be standing in moderately fresher air.

Before he moved down into the crowd he took note of a dark cloud waddling across the sky towards the city. There was the heavy scent of rain preceding it. Looking over the heads of the passers-by he spied a Hansom down the Strand.

He took out his pocket watch and made a mental calculation that a horse drawn Hansom would get him home before the heavens opened. Then raising his umbrella to catch the driver's eye, he called it over. The driver touched the brim of his hat and moved forward to meet him.

The only problem now was getting to it through the river of people before him. Men in top hats and bowlers crowded the pavement, many carrying heavy briefcases and their ubiquitous umbrellas. Their heads bowed slightly, so as not to accidentally make eye contact with one another. Rather than push his way through the crowd, James was forced to wait before he could cross to the street. The driver was a patient man and waited for him without complaint.

A man tried to engage the cab, but the driver said loudly enough to be heard over the crowd, "Sorry sir. There's a gentleman there what called me over, so I have to take 'im."

James felt an instant sympathy for the man who would take him home and was moved to be friendly towards him when they spoke. Strangely enough, the press of bodies had created a barrier to the volume of sound from the street which became almost painful when he reached the curb.

A parade of vehicle of all kinds brand descriptions moved by at an alarming rate, with a single police constable at the centre of the intersection directing the chaos along the busy Strand. The world had changed so drastically with the advent of the motorcar that city life still seemed utterly hopeless to James.

The stench of the horses and their droppings was something he could deal with, but the heat and smell of burning oil generated by those metal monsters was too much. The streets seemed filthier now with the litter carelessly cast off, and stains of motor oil and coal soot that blackened the cobblestones.

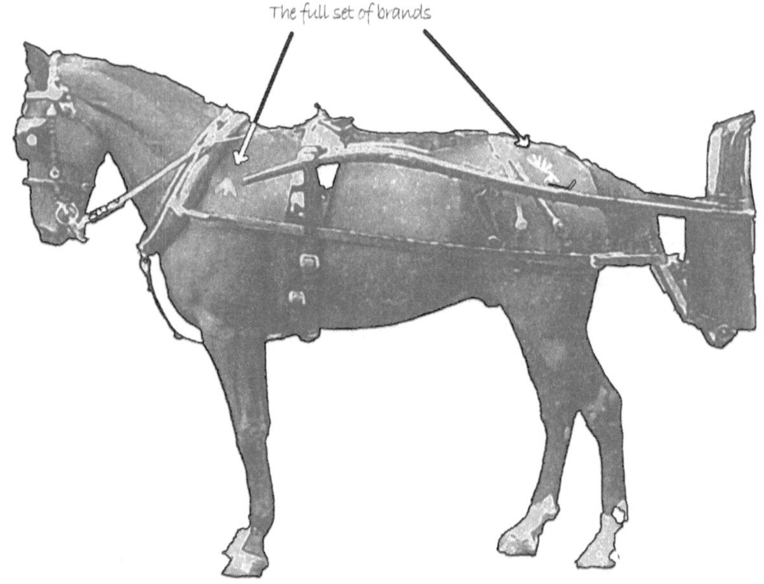

The War Horse

But then, even as a boy he thought walking the streets of London was a challenge to the senses.

The instant the horse came to a halt in front of him, he saw the marks branded on the shoulder and hip of the horse, the brands of the British Army. The poor old fellow looked as drawn and tired in that civilian harness as he must have looked on the plains of South Africa. The coincidence momentarily took his breath away. "Are you unwell gov?" the driver asked.

"Pardon?" Though it was quite warm James was shivering with that surge of adrenalin one gets when the level of excitement builds.

"Oh. Uh… no, I'm quite well thank you." He clambered in and pulled the comforter across his legs.

"I am relieved to hear it." The driver said, and pulled the door closed. "Then where am I taking you, governor?"

"Of course, excuse me. Number 5 Warwick Square."

"As good as done. Hup Jim!"

The horse trotted off and James let the clip-pity clop of it's hooves fill the silence, until he simply had to satisfy his curiosity.

"Driver."

"Yes gov."

"About your horse."

"If you're buying, I ain't selling."

"No-no, I…"

"Just funnin' with ya, sir. You was looking at them brands, weren't ya, sir. Yeays, people is always asking me about 'em, they are. Fact is, I 'ave no idea about what they mean."

"As it happens, I do."

"You're joking."

"Not at all. But first, would you mind telling me how you came by him?"

"Well, there's a bit of tale in that, I'll tell ya.

"I bought this 'orse down at the docks, I'd say it was ten or twelve years ago now. Oh, he was pretty sickly at the time, poor thing. Nearly starving he was. So I says to the man, 'Oy, I'll give ya a pound for 'em.' 'Three-pounds,' he says to me. Don't be daft I tells 'em, I'd be lucky to get 'im home before he drops. One pound-ten, and that's my final offer. He took it just like that. Best investment I ever made."

"Indeed," said James, and thought about that transaction and what it must have meant to this sad, brave animal.

"If you'd 'ave the story behind them brands, I'd be plenty chuffed, I would. Wouldn't it be sumping marvellous if I could elucidate my clients on its prominence."

Thankfully, they could not see each other, for James had to smile at the driver's interesting vocabulary. "Well then, be of good cheer." James took a moment to compose the history in his mind. "I suppose you might say that it began in the Canadian west."

"Well, imagine that. The wild west, land of the Mounties."

"Yes, he was bred in a territory called Alberta. The ranchers there raise the most wonderful horses, sturdy, dependable, built for the rugged conditions we faced in South Africa. The British Army bought them by the thousands to provide mounts for our troops."

"You're talking of the Boer War, sir?"

"I am indeed, and a terrible brutal affair that was on both man and beast. More than a hundred thousand horses died of wounds or disease during those years. Now, that upward pointing arrow you see on his shoulder, that marked him as the property of the British Army.

"The first one on his hip pointing down indicated that he was wounded, or fell ill, and was to be sold for meat."

"Merciful God!"

"I suppose in this case, God was somewhat merciful, though the horse went through hell to find his way to your cab. I noticed the scar on his flank. He had been shot out from under his rider, who most probably was felled by another bullet."

"Poor bugger."

"Yes." That thought delayed the story for a moment. "Uh... As it happened, that brand was not the sentence of certain death one would have imagined. Those Canadian horses were prized above all others on both sides of the war.

"Your old fellow was saved and restored to health by a Boer soldier, in need of a good mount. They were able to salvage many animals that we discarded. The forward pointing arrow testifies to that miracle."

"And the last one pointing up, what did that mean?"

"That brand declares that he was reclaimed by our side, and that most likely the Boer who rescued him had fallen in battle. But here is what puzzles me. I was under the impression that all the horses were destroyed at the end of the war. Your beast is living proof that there were a few English soldiers with hearts of gold who managed to smuggle their steeds back home."

Brought home by Hansom cab

"Or by the condition he was in when I found 'em, near starved to death 'e was. Some black hearted buggers crated 'em up down there to ship back to London and sell to the knacker's yards, or cabbies like me."

"That would be closer to the truth."

"Well, I appreciate the story, gov, and I thank you kindly for it."

"You are most welcome." He was still a fine horse, able to make good time from Earl's Court to Pimlico.

While paying the fare James heard a motorcar's brakes squeal to a stop at the end of the street. He ignored it on principle.

The idea of taking the fine old Hansom cabs off the streets to replace them with shiny metal and smelly engines was, in his view, monstrous and reprehensible. Yes, he knew that he was just another old soldier tilting at windmills, but this wave of modernity that was rolling over the island had come at a cost. So he ignored it and the passenger who stepped out of it before the car drove away.

There was a lesson to be learned from that act of defiance. Ignoring that particular machine, and its purpose for being there, was a mistake that would carry James to the very edge of death.

*****

CHAPTER ~ 2

THE LADY FROM SWITZERLAND

Before he managed to reach the sanctuary of his house a woman called to him. "Excuse me sir, am I addressing, Colonel James Wilson Horn, the eminent detective?" Adding the word 'eminent' was tantamount to gilding the lily, he thought, but he would accept it. He resented the interruption and for a brief moment entertained the idea of turning her away, but then politely asked, "May I be of some assistance to you madam?"

Miss Jennifer Butterworth

"I dearly hope that you can. I must confess that I followed you here all the way from the offices of Young, Thurborn, Davidson, and Hardcastle."

He was incredulous. "Did you? Whatever for?"

"Please forgive my impertinence. The thing of it was you see, I had some business there with the solicitor, Mr. Hardcastle, and I was having the most dreadful time deciding if I should go in or run away home and forget the whole thing. But then I saw you leaving the building, and I thought... perhaps..." she paused, uncertain.

"Yes?" he pressed.

"I recognized you from your photo in the Globe just last week and I..."

"And having seen my image in a newspaper, you decided to ignore your appointment with Mr. Hardcastle, and instead, chase across town after me?"

"No! Ah... well, yes," she admitted. James chose not to comment. "But I had to talk with you on a most peculiar, and desperate personal matter."

"A personal matter? My dear lady," he declared, as he rolled his umbrella, "what could possibly be so desperate?"

"Were you a friend of my late brother Bart?"

"I beg your pardon?" he said, coming to a full stop on the last steps to his front door He was trying to decide if he was conversing with a mad woman. "Madam, as we have not been introduced I have no idea who you are, so how could I possibly claim friendship with a man whom..." He stopped as he realised to whom he was speaking. "Gracious me, how utterly fantastic, you are the sister of Bartholomew Bigelow Butterworth."

"Jennifer Butterworth, yes."

"How utterly extraordinary. Only having just been apprised of your existence, and then here you are in the flesh. Do forgive my rudeness, Miss Butterworth. Please, will you come on up." He extended his hand, and as she took it, he said, "I fear the rain will begin any second now."

"For a moment, I thought you would be turning me away. Thank you, Colonel Horn. Frankly, without you, I can't imagine what I would do next."

"Good heavens my dear, under the circumstances how could I refuse you?."

"You have my thanks."

As he opened the door the most delicious smell of fresh bread and biscuits filled his senses. It seemed to calm him.

Miss Butterworth parked her umbrella along with his in the stand by the door, then stepped inside

"Your visit is well timed, Mrs. Findley is a fine baker." He rapped on the apartment door to his left and called out, "Anthony, we have a visitor." Then he crossed the hall to rapped again, on the door to his right. "Mrs Findley, I smell shortbread. Does that mean we will have tea in my study?"

The door opened instantly almost banging him on the nose, and a pleasant looking woman appeared dressed in a white blouse and black skirt, protected by a frilly white apron, the uniform of the housekeeper. "Yes, as it happens, I put on the kettle as soon as I saw you speaking to the young lady out on the street," her eyes sparkled with delight. "I thought we might be having company."

He assisted Miss Butterworth with removing her coat then Mrs. Findley took it saying,. "I'll take care of that for you." "Thank you."

"You are quite welcome."

James knocked on Anthony's door again, "I say, Anthony, wake up old boy. We have a guest."

A moment later the door opened and a rather dozy looking fellow with a handsomely trimmed moustache and beard appeared. "What is it James? I was taking a..." And upon latching eyes upon the lovely woman, he smiled broadly, "Oh, hello there. What an unexpected pleasure."

"I am sorry to barge in like this, but I have come to ask for Colonel Horn's assistance on a personal matter."

"Is that so?" He paused, as he looked from Miss Butterworth to James expectantly. "James?"

"What?" From James' questioning look it was that he was unsure of Anthony's meaning.

"Typical. Please forgive my elderly partner." Using his finger, he gave James a friendly poke on the shoulder. "I'm afraid he was too long on the veld and has forgotten his manners."

"Oh, for heaven's sake. My apologies. May I present my friend, Major Anthony Hillman."

She smiled and offered him her slender hand. "No, it is I who should apologize. I was acting rashly on the spur of the moment."

"Don't give it a thought, right James?"

"Of course. Anthony is familiar with my inquiries, so if it is alright with you I would like him to be part of our discussion in my study?"

"Oh," she flashed a nervous smile at Anthony once again, "of course."

"Good. Shall we go through and get acquainted while Mrs. Findley brings our tea?"

"Thank you." James proceeded down the wide hallway of the elegant town-home. Ornate Persian carpets lay like colourful islands of geometric design on the dark oak floor. Simply framed photos of James and Anthony in India and Africa filled the left wall as if they were open portals onto their past.

The large chamber at the back of the house was unquestionably a room decorated for a man, smelling of sweet pipe tobacco and furniture polish. The horns of antelope and gazelle, and the head of a buffalo were displayed above the mahogany shelves on the left side and front wall.

Those shelves were filled with books, treasures, and artefacts from the countries where James had served.

Another bookcase framed the casement window at the back, a mahogany and brass campaign desk and chair set occupied the space by the window alcove. But what stood out for her was a series of handsome paintings and drawings to her right. They were done by an artist she didn't recognize. "What a charming room," she said.

James smiled appreciatively as he offered her a seat in the Gainsborough armchair by the fire. "Thank you." He took its twin and Anthony secured a place at the end of the chocolate-leather chesterfield. Through the open window the refreshing fragrance of Mrs. Findley's roses wafted in with the breeze and carried the slight tangy taste of the rain that was falling on the garden.

"What divine little watercolours you have," she said, and gazed around at the wealth of interesting things. "And the drawings too, they are quite marvellous, Colonel Horn. They appear to be all by the same artist. You are obviously quite taken by this person's work, are you a collector?"

"No, I am the artist."

With a look of wonder she asked, "Truly?" He nodded. "Oh Colonel Horn, you are too modest, they're quite wonderful."

"Very kind of you to say so."

"Every spare moment offered him is filled with a painting or sketches like those. We must have hundreds about the place and he won't part with a single one. Frankly I'm thrilled to be the beneficiary of his talent."

James was thoroughly pleased with her interest in the works, and Anthony's continued support, though he showed little expression of it. He simply folded his hands on his lap and waited to hear her reason for the visit.

She seemed to be at a loss, so as the silence drew on Anthony decided to end it. "Pray Miss Butterworth, what brings you here?"

Mrs. Findley chose that moment to enter with the tea cart. "Here we are Colonel Horn, a fresh pot of tea and a batch of my famous shortbread." James had a feeling that she had been listening at the door and perhaps had thought she might be allowed to stay to hear the lady's story.

"Thank you Mrs. Findley, Anthony will pour." James' pronouncement quashed those hopes, and he waited for her to grasp the fact that it was a cue for her to depart.

As soon as she left and closed the door they began. "Now then, I must confess that I began looking into the story of your brother's death purely out of curiosity. The odd epitaph and symbol on the stone intrigued me. But clearly, with your arrival I see that there is more to it than I had thought. It would be immeasurably helpful for Anthony and myself, to understand in detail what led up to your brother's death."

After taking a sip she set it aside, "I wish I knew gentlemen, but apparently I have no more information about that than you do."

"And that was why you have come to London, to find out what had happened to him?"

"Yes, it was."

"But your brother died more than a year ago," said Anthony. "I don't understand. Why have you waited until now to come?"

"I didn't realize that he had died until very recently, that it is why I have come to you."

"I see."

"The truth of the matter is that I know almost nothing at all about my brother other than he started some sort of gentleman's club and then purchased a commission in the army. Since being sent off to Cambridge, he and I have corresponded infrequently.

As for what sort of person he had become, who his friends were, or what he had done before the war, I couldn't say. Except that he went through money as quickly as the water flows down the Thames."

James picked up the questioning. "How extraordinary." Both he and Anthony were puzzled by her statement. "Was there some particular occurrence that caused the split between you?"

"In short, our father's money. I have lived apart from my family for most of my life, much of it in Geneva. Bart and I were never on good terms; he would write newsy letters from Eton in response to mine, but that would only happen perhaps once or twice a year. Then after he left Eton, Bart wrote only to ask for money. Being the dutiful sister, I would write to say that I had placed the money in his account."

"I see. Moving on, there is a question Miss Butterworth that I must put to you now. You said you only just heard about his death."

"Yes."

"Whilst in Mr. Hardcastle's office, I saw a letter addressed to you, informing you of your brother's death. Did you receive such letter from him?"

"Yes I did."

"Thank you. Now, if you will pardon me for a moment, as Anthony mentioned a moment ago, he died in January of 1913, and yet you are only now acting upon the information in that letter. Why is that? Was the animosity you mentioned the reason it took you so long to come to London?"

"No, it most certainly was not." She opened her handbag and produced an envelope and handed it to him. "I received Mr. Hardcastle's letter just over a week ago. You can see that by the London post mark."

James was astonished. "Yes I see it." He showed it to Anthony.

"It was posted on June 12, 1914."

"If you look inside," she continued, "you will find that the letter is dated January 11, 1913."

"This is indeed the same letter I saw this morning. How curious."

"Then you will understand my hesitancy to act on my own."

"Indeed."

"Good. Then I am very glad to have come to you. What I wish to know is, how it is possible that a letter could be delayed for seventeen months? Was it lost in the mails? Or was it withheld from me? And if the latter is the case, then why?"

"Because of the perfect condition of the envelope and the date of the postmark, I would say that it had been withheld. Quite possibly at its source, the office of the man who wrote it. I have talked with Hardcastle at length and feel sure that he would not have had any part in this."

Anthony thought to ask an unusual question. "Tell me, is this the only notice of his death that you have received?"

Obviously, from her reaction she had been waiting for that question. "As it happens, no. I received the first in 1902."

"Excuse me, you said 1902?"

"Yes, it was from my father after he received one from the War Office informing him that Bart was wounded in battle and taken prisoner by the Boer. Another reported that he disappeared from the prison camp and as he failed to return to his unit and his body was never recovered, he was presumed to have died."

"Then the letter from Mr. Hardcastle must have come as quite a shock."

"No at all."

"But you thought him dead years ago."

"Yes, the story we heard was factual as far as the War Office was concerned. But, eight years later I found out that Bart was still alive."

"Beg pardon?"

"Yes, I received a curt letter from him, and just as before, he was asking for money. As I was apparently little more than a bank to him, I wasn't sure whether to be relieved or disappointed, frankly. He simply demanded that I reinstate his yearly stipend and make it retroactive to 1902. That came to a flat sixty thousand, and he wanted it all at once."

Anthony was floored. "You are joking of course."

"No."

"So, you are saying that he received ten thousand pounds a year? And that wasn't enough?"

"I would have thought that his being alive for eight years and saw fit to keep it a secret from me might have surprised you, but yes, he received ten thousand a year. He gave no explanation for his disappearance, nor for what he had been doing during the eight years he had been presumed dead."

James shared Anthony's surprise. "And you agreed to this?"

"I had no reason not to. If the man was alive it was his money. It made no difference to me."

"I now have no difficulty understanding how you must have felt."

"Thank you for that, Colonel Horn. Mr. Hardcastle's letter was shocking, but not entirely for the reason you may expect. As Mr. Hardcastle's was not the first letter, neither was it the last."

She revealed a second envelope. "This came to me on the very same day as that one."

"The more I hear, the stranger this mystery becomes. May I?"

She handed it to him. James inspected the envelope. "May I read its contents?"

"By all means," she said, and waited patiently for his comments.

When he was done he lowered the page slowly to his lap and stared out the window deep in thought. When he looked back again he said, "It is signed, a friend. Do you have friends in London?"

"Not a one."

"By God, the cruel intention of this letter is monstrous. The man is toying with you." He lifted the letter again and read from it, 'If you wish to know the truth about your brother's death, then come to London immediately.' This did not come from a friend." He folded it and replaced it in its envelope before tossing it on the side table. "I'd like to keep both letters for a while, If I may."

"Of course."

"He has written some instructions for you to follow. Have you done as he asked?"

"I have, but I haven't been contacted by anyone yet."

"That is more telling than you may think," James said, and Anthony caught the tone of urgency in his voice. "You say you saw me at the offices of Mr. Hardcastle."

"Yes."

"And you were there for an appointment?"

"No, I was going to go in unannounced to demand that he tell me what was going on. But I lost my nerve. I had gone twice before but was afraid to go in to confront the man."

"Your instincts may have spared you."

"What are you saying? You think he intends to kill me?"

"I beg your pardon; I did not mean to give you that impression. No, not Mr. Hardcastle. And I doubt that the man who wrote that detestable letter meant to harm you either. At least not yet. Had that been his plan then I dare say you would already be dead.

No, he wanted you here, that too is certain. The intent of having both letters arrive simultaneously was to make sure that you would come. The instructions were to make it possible for you to be found and watched."

"Watched? Whatever for?"

"Since your brother's suicide..."

"Excuse me! You said suicide?"

"You didn't know?"

"No! No one said anything about him killing himself."

"Then I am very sorry. With the second letter talking about the truth surrounding his death, I had assumed that you knew. I apologize. But now that you know, I am able to say freely that the motive behind the second letter was extortion."

"You honestly believe that?"

"I do now, yes. Let me suggest for a moment that your brother was in debt to this man; the nature of the debt is unimportant now but since he is dead and can no longer pay his debt this blaggard has gone to you."

"I can't imagine a debt so large as he could not honour it. I was giving Bart £10,0001 a year."

"I agree. That is an extraordinary sum indeed, Miss Butterworth and yet he was constantly asking for more."

"Bart was terrible with money. I must confess that I paid no attention to it at all. What he did with his life didn't interest me in the least."

"How is it that you are able to provide him with this seemingly inexhaustible supply of money?"

"I control my late father's businesses from Geneva. When he died, he left his entire estate to me with the exception of a few specific bequests to my brother and out stepmother."

[£10,000 a year in 1914 would be the equivalent of £1,229,463.84 in 2022]

"Butterworth Shipping! Of course, your father was Hollister Butterworth. Good grief, my mind must be addled to have taken so long to put you and the Shipping company together. It must be worth millions."

"In truth, it is and growing larger all the time." She took a deep breath, then sketched out the bitter story of wealthy family's tragedy. Of how their mother had died during childbirth. How she and her brother were raised by their beautiful, yet vapid stepmother and that she and her stepmother never got along.

She detailed how the building animosity between herself, the stepmother and the stepmother's favourite child, had become so fraught with fighting and angry words that eventually the father had to separate the twins and send them away. At the tender age of seven, Jennifer was placed in a school in Switzerland, never to return home and destined never to meet her brother again.

Following the dramatic unfolding of the Butterworth history, there was little doubt that the motive behind the letters and the mysterious headstone markings, was a plan fostered over time to extort money from the wealthy heiress over some dark family secret. She, of course, would not confirm that there was any truth to that theory. But it now came down to James and Anthony to find the man behind the plot and see that he is stopped. "I think you would be wise to hire a bodyguard," Anthony said.

"I already have. He is the man driving my motor car."

James paced the floor as he thought and the more he paced the more concerned Jennifer became. "What are you thinking?"

"Yes, sorry." He stopped pacing and went back to the mantle. "Some considerable effort has been made specifically to bring you here. Why? Was that his aim? He could have just as easily set upon you in Switzerland."

"A good question, James," said Anthony.

"Yes, quite." He took a moment to revisit his conversation with Mr. Hardcastle, then returned his attention to Jennifer, as another thought occurred. "This anonymous client of Hardcastle's based his plan on you being in a certain place at a certain time."

"A schedule that has, as you said, been running for over a year," Anthony said.

"Yes, with room for error. The person who dictated the first letter was most certainly the same man who sent the second. Why he went to such considerable effort to disguise his writing remains a puzzle. In any event, he asked you to place an ad in the social pages of the Daily News."

"Yes, and to say where I would be staying."

"Exactly, and as I had suspected, his intent was to set his trap with the solicitor's letter. Then some element of his plan was altered, the timing of an event, perhaps. Thus, he found it necessary to postpone its delivery. Seventeen months went by, and a new opportunity has presented itself. The first letter was mailed, but then he may have thought that a further inducement was necessary.

He began to pace again as his mind worked. "Perhaps he had discovered that you knew your brother's business affairs better that he did himself. That you would know that there was nothing to take care of and would refuse to make the trip. So to be sure you would come, he crafted the second letter. A tantalizing promise of truth, a suggestion that some unknown secret, a crime perhaps, would be revealed."

"I assure you, Colonel Horn, there is nothing from my past that requires coving up."

"Please, take no offense, it was merely a suggestion of what the man was thinking. You would have to come to find out what it was he had to sell."

He stopped at the fireplace and rested his elbow on the mantle again. Taking out his pipe as he spoke, he filled it, "Anthony, your thoughts?" Then struck a match.

"First my thought is that your brother did not end his own life, he was murdered."

"Good, Yes, yes, go on."

"My gut tells me that our man is not working alone. He would have to have some influence in the solicitor's office..."

"I think I know the man, yes."

"And presuming that he has confederates, then it would be safe to assume that she was spotted and just as she followed you, someone must have followed her. He could be outside the house at this very moment."

Anthony shot up from the chesterfield. "Did you ask your driver to park the automobile nearby?"

"Actually, I asked him to drive around the block and park in front of the house. Oh dear, that was a mistake, wasn't it?"

"Never mind that, it can't be helped now. This house could be under surveillance at this very moment."

Miss Butterworth's motorcar

"Anthony," James turned his full attention towards his friend, "could you see what you can do about that?"

"I'm on my way." Hillman left the room, collected his revolver and left by the back door.

****

A Spy In The Bush

The sky had grown very dark and the rain had begun in earnest as he sprinted through the garden. There was a lane at the back between their row of houses and the row on the next street over. Anthony was making his way to St. George Street when, as luck would have it, one of the neighbours was just preparing to take his dog out for a walk.

The poor old fellow looked positively miserable, hunched over the dog trying to get the leash untangled from his legs. Anthony knew that Fred disliked the dog intensely, but since it was like a child to his wife, he had to walk it twice a day.

"Say there, Fred, hello" Anthony called out as a brilliant idea sparked in his mind.

"Oh, is that you Anthony? What the devil are you doing out in this rain dressed like that?"

"Had a sudden urge to take a walk. Having trouble with Hector are you?"

"Blasted beast will drive me to drink, he will."

"As I am already out and wet, how about letting me take Hector for his walk this afternoon, and you can go back inside and get comfortable?"

"What, are you serious?" Anthony nodded with a sympathetic smile and the old man's face brightened measurably. Holding out the leash, he said, "You are a godsend my son, that's what you are. See that he does his business, will you?" The leash changed hands without forcing Anthony to slow down and with a little tug, the setter was quite happy to walk off with him.

Warwick Square was a broad boulevard with a wide park down the centre which was kept up by the residents. Looking about him to see if there was anyone else about, Anthony unlocked the gate mid-way along the street.

As a hunter breed, the dog wasn't bothered by the rain and they kept up a good pace. Sticking to the path, as most dog walkers did, he began going around counterclockwise until he was parallel to Belgrave Rd.

From there he could see to the far end of the park. And yes, there was a man stooped down at the fence directly across from number five, and it was quite obvious why he was there. They had the park to themselves, so Anthony made his approach.

Anthony walked by him and noticed the discarded cigarettes in the grass, a sure sign that the intruder had been there for some time.

"I say, you there, what is the meaning of this?"

"Eh?"

"I have never seen you before, have I?" He thought that playing the clueless resident was the best way to begin the confrontation. "You do realize that this is a private park, reserved for the residents of Warwick Square. Oh, we take a very dim view of trespassers here, my friend. Do you know what? I shall have to call for a policeman to see you off, that's what. How do you like that?"

"No, you don't, I'll leave when I'm good and ready."

The spy stood up to challenge Anthony. Sensing the danger, Hector immediately began barking, snarling and baring his teeth at the man. Anthony was quite impressed by his ferocity. The startled man stepped back, raising his arms defensively. "Hold your dog, I warn you."

"I will as long as you behave yourself." Hector was beginning to enjoy his new power and strained at the leash. "Easy old thing, it's alright." Miraculously, Hector stopped his act and sat down, surprising Anthony no end. "By your accent, I would say you are from the continent, Germany perhaps? I'm sure the authorities would be interested in your activities here." The intruder began looking for a way to escape. "What will it be then? Shall I call the police, or will you be a reasonable chap and quietly leg it?"

After a moment of indecision, he chose the easy way out and, giving Hector a wide birth, headed to the gate through which Anthony had come.

"A wise choice. I will be reporting this to the police with a full description, so may I suggest that you leave the area post haste?"

That should have been left unsaid, for the man chose instead to eliminate his witnesses. Reaching inside his coat for a gun, he turned on Anthony.

"That would be a profoundly bad idea," Anthony said, as he had already drawn his revolver and was pointing it at the man's chest.

The spy would not be put off, but before he could get off a shot, Anthony put a bullet through his heart, and that was the end of it. At that point the rain shower ended as if the gods had turned off the tap. In the distance he heard the policeman's whistle and then, from further off, another.

James and Miss Butterworth arrived before the police. Standing over the body James asked, "What the devil happened?"

"I offered him the option to leave peacefully. He gave me no choice."

"I have no doubt at all that this was justified."

That fateful moment in Warwick Park

James placed his hand on Anthony's shoulder to comfort him. Jennifer was standing well back but was listening intently to their conversation.

"Thank you. I think the danger facing our client is much greater than we could have imagined." At that point Jennifer moved closer.

"True, but as yet we have not had her permission to work on her behalf."

"Oh, dear me," she said eagerly, "yes of course. I was hoping you would take the case."

Her chauffeur joined them and was standing behind her, shielding her from the street. James noticed that he too had a gun in his hand.

"Then we are at your service, Miss Butterworth. Let me suggest that your driver put his weapon away before the bobbies get here. Also, I suggest that under no circumstances should you to return to the Bedford Hotel. Leave your things there, find another lodging at once, somewhere where you will be less conspicuous."

"Of course."

Let me know where you have landed, and we will arrange to have your belongings sent on to you."

"That is very kind, thank you."

Just then the first constable ran through the open gate along with one of the neighbours who heard the shot. "I heard shooting. What's going on?"

The constable stopped at the body and looked down at the hole in the dead man's chest as did the neighbour.

"Alright, alright sir, I'd advise you to step back if you please. Thank you kindly." He straightened up and looked about him. Addressing Anthony and James, as they were there when he came, "Now gentlemen, will one of you please explain why there is a dead man lying here?"

Still in control of the retriever, Anthony began to share the details, "I'm afraid I have just killed the man, constable."

"Yes, well I can see that, can't I?" Noting Anthony's attire and the dog. "Was there any particular reason for shooting him, sir, or were you just out for an evening hunt?"

"We suspected that someone might be spying on our house. I came out looking to see if I was correct. I caught him peering through the bushes over there and when I confronted him he drew his weapon."

"And am I to understand, sir, that you are still armed?"

"I am."

"Then I would feel easier, sir, if you would carefully hand the pistol to me. Grip first if you please."

Ignoring the policeman's conversation with Anthony, Miss Butterworth continued her discussion with James. "Not to be too presumptuous, but can you recommend such a place?"

"As it happens, I know of an inn near King's Cross, called the Shield and Arms."

Turning to her driver, "Jorgenson, would you be able to find that?"

"Yes Ma'am."

"Good. Then I shall take my leave of you, gentlemen and will telephone you once I am situated. I hate to be such a nuisance, but I will be in need of a change of clothes for this evening, so if it is at all possible...?"

"I will have it seen to at once," said James.

Before she withdrew to her motor car, Miss. Butterworth approached the constable. "Ah, excuse me for interrupting constable? Major Hillman, you may have just saved my life. I am most grateful to you, thank you."

"An honour, Ma'am."

"All done then, are we?" She nodded and withdrew. "Right. As you were saying, sir?"

"Yes, and when I asked him to leave he drew a weapon and was prepared to shoot me..."

"He was, was he?"

"He was, I'm quite certain about that. Us actually, I gather he didn't like the dog either." Looking down at the dog sitting quietly beside him.

The policeman raised an eyebrow. "And I suppose you are like one of them quick on the draw Americans."

"Uh... no. As I said before, I was expecting something like this and had my revolver ready before he turned on me."

"I see." He gazed down at the body as if to find his next question there. "And you did not know the gentleman?"

"Never saw him before in my life. By his accent, I'd say he was German."

****

FIELD MARSHAL EARL ROBERTS

On October 22nd of 1912, Field Marshal Earl Roberts gave a speech in Manchester in which he reminded the audience that Cobden and Bright's prediction that peace and universal disarmament would follow the adoption of free trade, had not happened. He went on to warn of the threat to the British Empire posed by Germany. From his perspective, he could see that Germany was diligently

Field Marshal Earl Roberts

preparing for war. He said, "Gentlemen, my fellow-citizens and fellow-Britishers, citizens of this great and sacred trust, this Empire, if these were my last words, I still should say to you - arm yourselves and if I put to myself the question.

"How can I, even at this late and solemn hour, best help England, - England that to me has been so much, England that for me has done so much? - again I say, Arm and prepare to acquit yourselves like men, for the day of your ordeal is at hand."

The Nation newspaper claimed Roberts had an "unimaginative soldier's brain" and that Germany was "a friendly power."

A soldier's brain perhaps, but history would prove that it was the writers for the Nation that lacked imagination.

*****

CHAPTER ~ 3

SCOTLAND YARD

After his interview with Miss Butterworth, it was imperative to bring what he had discovered thus far to the attention of the Metropolitan Police. The shooting in Warwick Square had already opened the door to that collaboration and he knew just the person with whom to collaborate, Superintendent Henry Dobbs at Scotland Yard.

Old Scotland Yard

After so much handling there was little chance of identifying anyone from fingerprints found on the letters' envelopes. Presumably Mr. Hardcastle, Miss Butterworth, he and Anthony were the only ones to have touched their contents. Perhaps the police could obtain a sample of fingerprints from the people who may have handled the envelope, if anyone of them had touched the letter itself, they would have a suspect. No, that would be impossible, as letter carriers and others from London to Geneva would have handled them.

Superintendent Dobbs was an old army friend that James had known during their days with army intelligence. They had worked under General Frederick Sleigh Roberts, who was then Commander-In-Chief, India and then continued under his command in South Africa.

Lord Roberts was responsible for bringing the science of fingerprints from India where it originated, to England and the rest of the Empire and America.

He also originated the idea of the concentration camps in South Africa, to isolate the Boer guerrilla fighters from their families. It was a harsh move made even more harsh when Lord Kitchener took over Commander-In-Chief. He expanded the camps and introduced the scorched earth policy creating food shortages, starvation and illness.

The new policies brought about a crisis of conscience, which eventually forced James, Anthony and Dobbs to resign their commissions. With the experience gained under Roberts, James and Anthony chose careers in the community as independent civilian detectives. Dobbs chose to employ his experience with the Metropolitan London Police. He thought that James had made a mistake in not joining the force as he did, but they continued as good friends.

James arranged for a visit and Dobbs said it was better late than never.

"Henry, good of you to see me at such short notice."

"Not a bit of it, James, nice of you to drop in dear boy, I will always have time for an old friend. Sherry?"

"Please." Dobbs handed him a handsome crystal with a generous serving of a very good Portuguese aperitif. "Thank you, Henry. Cheers."

"Cheers." They each sipped their sherry appreciatively. "Take a seat, James, and tell me what brings you to the Yard today?"

"You will recall my friend and partner, Anthony Hillman."

"Of course. A good chap, great agent."

"To be sure, we are working together again and yesterday he was involved in an unfortunate shooting. The other man died."

"You are speaking of the one in Warwick Square?"

"I am, so you have heard of it."

"Yes, as I recall the shooter…"

"That would be Anthony."

"As you say, Anthony has claimed self-defence."

"He has."

"It was all in the briefing I had this morning, didn't twig to Anthony's name though. As I recall, it involved a German trespassing in the park."

"He must have climbed over the fence."

"It hardly seems like the sort of thing which would result in a shooting. Should I attach any special significance to the man's nationality?"

"Other than what one reads in the press about what passes for international politics in Europe, I couldn't say. As to his reason for spying on my house, it was connected in some way to a mysterious death that we are currently investigating."

"Is that so? Is this new case something of which I should already have been briefed?"

"It is an old one actually, a case that the Yard closed over a year ago."

"And yet you have found a reason to open it again, something that we had missed."

"I am. It was a death attributed to suicide when in fact, I believe, it was pre-meditated murder."

"Really, are you sure?"

"Quite."

"And what might be the name of the deceased?"

"Bartholomew Bigelow Butterworth."

"Good heavens, now there is a mouthful." He paused to recollect. "That happened well over a year ago, I believe."

"A year-and -a-half ago, actually."

"Tempus does fugit eh? What was it that alerted you to our blunder?"

"It was quite by chance really. It began the other day when I came across something on a gravestone that caught my eye."

"Really. I can't imagine that you found a crime on a gravestone. How odd, James."

"I can't say that it was a crime, but yes, it was odd and disturbing, yet at the same time rather interesting."

"Do you spend much time studying gravestones?"

"Not a great deal of time, no. But our cemeteries offer a quiet place to walk. The reason that I mention it is the nature of the symbol I found carved on Butterworth's stone."

"Go on, what did this symbol look like? Was it something satanic perhaps?"

"No nothing like that." He drew it on a scrap of paper and handed it to his friend.

"It was the brand our army used during the war to signify that a horse had been sold off to the knackers, plus the mark the Boer used to claim the animal as their own."

"Uh hahhh, the intersecting arrows, yes I remember them. And what significance do you attach to it?"

"It was a gut feeling."

"I'm all for gut feelings, as long as they aren't due to indigestion."

"I thought it was the mark of a traitor."

"Oh yes, I see what you mean. Was he?"

"It is unclear at the moment. It began as a sort of puzzle and I was fitting the pieces together simply as a diversion. His death was attributed to suicide, but then someone presented a new chapter to the story which was so bizarre that it persuaded me that it might actually have been foul play. My conclusion is that it is, in fact, cold-blooded murder."

"Now James, that seems like quite a leap don't you think?"

"Perhaps, but now with the death of that German spy, the two letters my client received to inform her of her brother's death, the fact that they arrived on the same day after being posted seventeen months apart, I must say my supposition seems to be solidifying." James waited for a response, but Henry was still processing the information. "Consider this. The first letter asked her to attend to Butterworth's estate. It had already been processed. The second urged her to come to London to discover the truth. Clearly that suggested that Scotland Yard's conclusion of suicide was incorrect."

Dobbs' expression became very grave. "The press would be outrageously cheerful to spread the news of a police foul-up." He was reading the headlines even now. "Do you have the letters with you?"

"I do, the client's name is Jennifer Butterworth," he said, then handed him the letters, "but I must insist that you keep that to yourself. I have secreted her away in a safe location and the less notice drawn to her the better."

Dobbs' smile couldn't hide the official note in his voice. "I can do that for you James. Listen to me old friend I won't stop you from continuing your investigation, but if this is a case of murder then it is police business."

Appreciating the fact that Henry didn't push, James agreed. "Yes of course."

"There might be a chance of taking the fingerprints from both letters then, excluding yours, Anthony's, and Miss Butterworth's of course, we might find the killer. We could see if there are any that belong to the people we should come across during the course of our investigation."

"If you don't mind, Henry, I should like to stay in control of the case for now."

Henry studied his old comrade's expression, remembering the years of successful investigations the man had worked on, and said, "As you wish. Though James, the wig in the big office will not be pleased to be seen in a subordinate role in an ongoing criminal investigation."

"We will be as inconspicuous as possible, of course. Anthony and I will share everything we are able to uncover with you and it would be useful if the Yard will do likewise."

"We'll see." There was a non-committal answer if there ever was one. "Getting back to the letters for a moment. This one came from a solicitor..."

"Hardcastle, of... uh let me think. Yes, Young, Thurborn, Davidson, and Hardcastle."

"Oh yes, I know of them, a reputable firm. Has he explained to you the reason for its delay?"

"No not as yet, but I had planned to confront him following this meeting."

"Why not let us look."

"Certainly." Dobbs wrote a note.

"And the other?"

"We have no idea where that came from other than the post mark is London, dated two days prior to it being received."

"And they came together?"

"They did."

"An amazing coincidence, that."

"If one believes in coincidences."

"Quite. Alright, let me put it to you James. How would you like to proceed?"

James sat forward striking a more assertive posture, and said, "To fully understand the circumstances, I would like to view the evidence found during the investigation of Mr. Butterworth's death."

"I would expect nothing less, from you," Henry said as he lit a cigarette. "Tell me, how did you find your way from the carving on the gravestone to the solicitor who wrote the letter?"

"It was the epitaph that stung my curiosity at first. I wanted to find out who the devil would write such a thing."

"I am confused. I thought this was just about the mark on the stone."

"Indeed, that symbol irked me, but the script warranted an investigation."

"I can see that. An idle mind is the devil's playground and all that, but what was so rude as to cause you such distress?"

"Distress would have been too strong a word in the beginning, but it certainly has become stressful. It said, Brother, Betrothed, Bastard."

"You're joking?"

"Not at all. Now you see the reason for my curiosity. The words and the symbol are linked, their meaning is the puzzle to be solved."

"You have always been incurably curious."

"Yes, I should like to believe that I have. And having found Mr. Hardcastle to be the author of that first letter, I returned home, only to discover that I had been followed by a young woman."

"Miss Butterworth."

"Yes, she had followed my cab from Hardcastle's office."

"Could she have been following you since the cemetery?"

"I think I would have noticed her."

"Did you notice her following you?"

"Strangely, I did not."

"Well then James," he began, as he stood up to replenished James' glass, "she could have been following you for days."

"Had that been the case then I rather think that I would have..."

"It seems that this rash indulgence has blown up in your face, my friend."

"Yes," he sighed, "it would appear so."

"Buck up old sport." A thought occurred to him. "Here, let me call up DS Willows, he was the man who would have investigated Butterworth's death."

"Thank you."

"Don't mention it dear boy." After putting the bottle down, he picked up the telephone earpiece. "Delighted to help in any way I can." He tapped on the hook. "Uh... yes, would you have Detective Sergeant Willows come to my office please, and ask him to bring the Butterworth file with him. Thank you."

He replaced the instrument in its cradle then looked back at James. "Do you know him?"

"We have had some dealings in the past."

"I understand that he can be off-putting at times." Dobbs said. "Where was I? Oh yes, more sherry?"

"Yes thanks, just a drop." He watched as Henry filled the glass with the rich golden wine, then set the glass down on his side table. "Off-putting might be one of the kinder things I would say about the man."

"Really, I am sorry to hear that. In my experience, he has always been a most respectful officer." He replaced the decanter on the credenza and returned to his desk. Presently there was a knock at the door. "Come."

Already a heavy man, DS Willows had added some tonnage since their last encounter. "You called for me, sir? Oh ... it's you is it? What's 'e 'ere for, sir? Finally crossed the line, has he?"

"A pleasure as always, Willows," James lied.

The ruddy faced copper trundled in with all the grace of a swaggering hippopotamus. He removed his bowler hat and held it under his arm like a helmet. Henry's usual pleasant demeanour had immediately turned chilly. "Close the door."

Sensing the sudden change in the senior officer's attitude he stiffened slightly. "Yes sir. Sorry sir." He returned to the door and closed it carefully. Turning again he made his way back to Dobbs' desk without comment.

"DS Willows, Lieutenant Colonel James Horn is one of my oldest friends. I suggest that in the future you will offer him the same level of respect as you do me. I hope I have made myself clear."

"You have sir, yes. Good morning Mr. Horn." He could have stopped there but his nature prodded him on to one more insult.

"Didn't I just read about you in the Globe?"

With eyebrows lifted to maximum Dobbs turned to James. "Did he?" Then back to Willows who, having scored a point, was now beaming. "James, I have never known you to seek the public's attention."

James said nothing, thinking it must have been Anthony who sought the attention. In fact, without informing James, Anthony had spoken to the press and even supplied the photographs.

"How very interesting." And since James remained silent, Dobbs looked back to his sergeant for more information. "Well man, what was it about?"

"You remember Jeffrey Pims, sir. Done 'is wife and the nanny with a shotgun then scarpered with the child."

A light of recognition shown from Dobbs' eyes. "Oh yes. Lord knows what drove him to it."

James felt compelled to supply the information that the Lord could not. "The fiend was seeing another woman and had been heard to say that if he could get rid of his wife he'd be a happy man. And that just was what he did. The children's nanny was an unfortunate witness to the murder."

"Then he'll swing for sure," said Dobbs. "How did you nab him?"

Willows chose to impart that bit of the story. "Oh, your friend, Mr. Horn, sir, he 'ad hiself quite a romp, didn't he?" His contempt was obvious. "Chased that murdering sod all the way down t' Dover. Of course, my boys would 'a nicked him long before he got out of London. Ain't that right Mr. Horn?"

"I suppose they would have Sergeant Willows had they been on the job instead of cracking innocent heads," James said mildly.

"Oy, …"

"Then it was a good job he was caught, eh Willows. Well done James," the Superintendent said, putting the man in his place once again.

"Yes sir."

"Have you brought the Butterworth case file?"

"Yes sir." He placed it in front of the Superintendent, then stood back from the desk. "There weren't nothing unusual about it as far as I could see. Death caused by a self-inflicted gunshot to the head. The man done himself, sir."

Curious, James asked, "Where in the head did he shoot himself?"

"Where? What kind of a question is that?"

"I am asking for the specific location on the head of the victim where he placed the gun. Did he shoot himself through the mouth, under the chin, or in the temple?"

"What does that matter, 'e killed 'is-self."

"Yes, you said that, but do try to humour me, please."

"O'right, 'e put the gun behind his ear, 'appy now?"

"How could one be happy when talking about suicide? You recorded the physical evidence, did you?"

"I see. You wants t' dot the 'I's and cross the 'T's. Well, let me 'elp you with that Mr. Horn." He took out his notebook, licked his unwashed thumb and pushed back through a year-and-a-half's worth of notes scribbled on lined pages. "The body was discovered in the Collections Room at 'is club at…"

"What club would that be?" James asked.

"Eh? uh… Oh, let me see," Willows was made more unhappy by the interruption and being forced to turn back a page. "O'right, 'ere it is. It were Club 17, 17 Catherine Place."

"Interesting," he said.

"You know the club, sir?"

"I have heard mention of it, please continue."

"The club's porter heard the shot and come down running from his flat, found the body in the chair and called it in."

"What time of day was this?"

"Time? Um... Uh..." Finding his place on the page he regrouped and started again. "It were... let me see... uh... the call come in at 2:12 am. We arrived at the scene ten minutes lay'er and proceeded to..."

James interrupted him again. "So, in addition to the porter's flat, there are guest rooms at the club?"

"What? ... Yeah, four of 'em."

"Do we know why Mr. Butterworth was staying at the club?"

Willows lost his temper. "Now, how would I know that?"

"It seems to me that it was a reasonable question Detective Sergeant," said Dobbs. "Answer it if you can."

"Sorry sir, I don't know."

"You might have asked someone, I suppose," James said, with mild sarcasm. "Isn't that how one would normally conduct an investigation?"

"If I may continue..."

"No, hang on for just a moment please, Detective Sergeant," said Dobbs. "Who found him?"

"The porter found the body, sir."

"Yes you said that, but what I wanted is his name, Willows."

"Oh, sorry sir. Uh..." he consulted his notes, "It's Fry, sir. Mr. Archie Fry."

"Thank you. James..." he began, but James interrupted him.

"Willows, would that be Archie Fry, by any chance?"

"Yes, I believe it is."

"Henry, do you recall a Sgt. Archibald Fry in the SIS office in Johannesburg? The man with the incredible memory. Nothing slipped by the man."

"Oh yes, I remember the man, frightening to think what that man could recall."

"Yes. If it is the same man then he would be an invaluable witness. Let me ask you Willows, where was the body found?"

"In the Collections Room, on the second floor."

"And Sgt. Fry's room is where?"

"His flat is on the top floor."

"I see, and how many floors are there?"

"At last count there was five. Now, do you 'ave any other questions, or may I continue?"

"First, let me picture the geography of the place."

"If you must," the detective growled.

"Yes, thank you." Clearly James was enjoying the detective's discomfort. "Now you said, Mr. Fry was in his rooms upstairs. Presumably he was asleep when the shot was fired."

"I suppose."

"It woke him, and he realised that it had come from somewhere below."

"O' course 'e did. There weren't nothin' above 'im, were there?"

"Quite so. And, he would have had to scramble from his bed, shake the cobwebs loose, pull on his house coat and slippers. Then unsure of where the sound of the shot had come from, he would have had to search all the rooms on each floor until he found the body in the Collections Room. Does that sound about right Willows?"

"If you say so."

"Is there a telephone in the Collections Room?"

"No, there is only one telephone, in the Porter's office, main floor."

"Then, Mr. Fry would have had to run down another flight of stairs to make the call, wouldn't he?"

"I suppose so, yes."

"There is no supposing DS Willows, if he made the call then he would have had to go down to his office to do it. Yes?"

"Yes, sir."

"That must have taken him several minutes, would it not?"

"I suppose it would have, sure, but..."

"When you asked Mr. Fry how long he searched before he found the body, and then how long it took him to call it in, what did he say?"

"He didn't say, because I didn't have to ask him, did I? Like I said, the man killed himself. What did it matter how long it took the ruddy porter to find the body and then call us?"

"I see," said James.

"Now can I continue?"

Henry Dobbs was fascinated by how James was reconstructing the sequence of the events. It was obvious that Willows had overlooked several details which could have led him to an entirely different conclusion.

"Yes, by all means."

"That's all what there was to it, sir. I can't add anything to what was written down in my notes. It's all in the file there, sir. Mr. Horn can read it all for his-self. There wasn't anything out the ordinary about it, sir."

"I see, very well Detective Sergeant. Does that satisfy you James?"

"Apart from completely disagreeing with his conclusions, he has given me all the information I needed. Thank you Willows."

"Then we seem to have covered it nicely," Dobbs said "Thank you Willows. That's all for now."

"Yes sir." Replacing his bowler, he strode to the door and let himself out.

"Well it is plain to see that he'll not be sending you a card at Christmas, eh James?"

"One must be grateful for small blessings."

"Yes, very small blessings indeed," Dobbs said and James smiled. "You certainly showed him for a fool and he won't soon forget it. Do you always test people like that?"

"No, just those that irritate me."

"Right, well I have to splash my shoes, so take your time with the file and I'll return in say … twenty minutes. Would that be enough time?"

"I should think so. Many thanks Henry." The photos told the story Willows failed to mention. There was a newspaper on the floor covered by blood splatter, and the splatter extended almost to the far side of the room where the bullet was lodged. There was splatter behind the chair as well, but there was no silhouette to show with any clarity, that someone had stood behind the victim when the shot was fired. That, however, didn't rule out the possibility that the assassin had used it to protect himself.

The attitude of the body, thought James, was the key factor in proving it was murder. He was slumped in the chair with his chest on the arm rest, his face looking straight down at the floor, and his left arm hanging to the right of his legs. That and the direction of the blood splatter told James that Butterworth had been looking back to the right side when he was shot. His position in the chair, the pattern of gore on the newspaper which lay directly in front of the chair, all came together to prove conclusively that he had been shot from behind.

And as there was no sign of defensive wounds, it was likely that he had been surprised by his killer. He turned to see him and then was shot.

His time was up as Dobbs re-entered the room. "Have you solved the case?"

"For the moment all I have proven beyond a doubt, that it was murder," He dropped the photographs on the desk as he stood up. "What those photographs showed me was that the killing was pure theatre."

"What?"

"It was all staged by the killer to make it look like suicide, but he made four glaring errors."

"Did he really?"

"I believe so," said James. "If his point was to have us find a clue in the newspaper, he should have found a way to connect it without spilling a bloody mess all over it. As there were no pictures which focused specifically on the newspaper, whatever significance it may have had was lost."

"I see, good point."

"The second discrepancy was that no one could hold that gun behind his ear to shoot himself. The arm and shoulder simply do not allow for that movement, especially when one is sitting in a wing back chair. Third, from the trajectory of the shot, it would mean that the victim would have to be turned in the chair and looking to his right. I can't believe that a man about to do himself in, would choose such an uncomfortable pose in order to deliver the bullet. And finally, he chose the club as the location to do that imponderable deed, he chose a weapon from the club's gun collection, and he also laid the newspaper out at his feet. Having gone to all of that bother, why did he not leave a note to explain it all?"

"Yes James, I see your point." Henry tapped his front teeth with the end of his matchstick.

"Thank you Henry. Altogether, these facts tell me that there was a specific purpose for shooting the victim that way and that is now the mystery that we must solve."

It took less than two minutes to convince his friend that DS Willows was a complete buffoon. "The Metropolitan Police will have to do a much better job than this in the future if our aim is to apprehend the criminals."

"You might start by replacing Willows."

"A suggestion that I will take up with the Senior Superintendent after lunch."

James had been considering his next move with care, and it seemed that his investigation must continue at Club 17. "And, after lunch I will consider the best way to approach the porter of Club 17 to find out what's going on there."

"Cross-checking the facts, eh? Same old James, you haven't changed a bit. Once you get hold of the bone you'll gnaw on it till it's gone. I dare say if you and I had stuck it out with old Kitchener, you might have ended the war years earlier."

"Perhaps." James smiled.

"And I would have taken all the credit."

With that James actually laughed. "I suppose neither of us has changed much over the years. You will let Willows down gently, won't you?"

"Not on your life. The man deserves a great thumping boot applied to his backside. It was downright sloppy police work."

"Indeed, well thank you so much for your assistance today, Henry. It has been wonderful to see you again."

"An absolute pleasure, James. It has been such a treat to have this time with you. I had forgotten what a good fellow you are to have around."

"How kind of you to say."

"I would thoroughly enjoy doing it again sometime. Let's make it soon, shall we, say lunch at my club?"

"I should like that," James said.

"Jolly good. I'll call you, shall I?"

"Please do." As James' footfalls echoed down the pavement away from Scotland Yard, his thoughts were of his next port of call, Club 17 and a conversation with Mr. Fry.

*****

CHAPTER ~ 4

CLUB 17

Number 17 Catherine Place was the perfect address for a social club of military gentleman. It was practically around the corner from Wellington Barracks, and well-nigh in the back yard of Buckingham Palace. Had James his druthers, he would have been quite happy to simply wander over there and continue his investigation that day, but it wasn't to be. He needed an invitation from a member to get through the door. Anthony would have to take charge of that detail.

To that point, Anthony made friends with a subaltern named Timothy Blackwood when they travelled through Salisbury, Rhodesia and following the protocol for acquiring assets, once acquired he introduced Blackwood to James over drinks in the Officer's Mess.

Gathering assets was never done without some purpose, and sometimes that purpose wasn't readily apparent at the time.

Intelligence is a long-term game and as luck would have it, that asset was now a member in good standing at Club 17.

Anthony wrote to him, to ask if he would be kind enough to put James and himself up for membership at his club.

Thrilled to be remembered, Timothy wrote back at once and said he would be honoured to have them join the club. A date was made for the following day to meet at half past one for lunch at the club and be introduced to some of the other members.

Armed with questions for Timothy and for Mr. Fry they arrived early and, as anticipated, were greeted at the door by Mr. Fry. Dressed in blues and greys of a retired soldier, he sported his old regimental tie and a chest full of medals from the South African war.

"Why if it isn't Lieutenant Colonel Horn. Hello sir, and Major Hillman. Well, upon my word, sirs, to see you two together after all these years."

The memory of this man flooded back. "Sergeant Fry isn't it. The man with the incredible memory."

"Yes sir. Good of you to remember me. May I shake your hand, sir?"

"Of course," James said, reaching for his hand without hesitation. "Old comrades, eh?"

"How very kind, sir." He beamed with pride. "My word sirs, it must be, what… nearly thirteen years now since we were in Cape Town."

"You look fit, how have you been?" Anthony asked.

"As well as can be expected, sir. I got married when I came home and now I'm back at work, I am. But never mind that, it is like old times now. You are here to see Captain Blackwood, aren't you?"

"We are," said James.

"Well sirs, come right this way and I'll let him know you are here."

He showed them into a small but comfortable sitting room where non-members were to wait for their appointments. "I'll send in the orderly to bring you some refreshments."

"Oh Fry, hang on a moment."

"Yes sir."

"Perhaps after luncheon we could get together and have a little reunion."

"Nothing could please me more, sir," he said, and as he hurried off, beaming. A young man came in with a silver tray upon which rested a box of Cubans, glasses, and a decanter of twenty-year-old whisky. The drink they accepted gladly, but they declined the cigars. Enjoying the single Malt, James mentioned that it felt as though they were the only ones in the building. "Is it always this quiet in the building?" he asked the attendant.

"As a matter of fact, it is, sir. It is so quiet here they tell me, that one night a man shot his self, up in the gallery and there was only old Mr. Fry what heard it."

"How extraordinary. When was that?"

"Oh, it must have been about a year and a half ago, I would think. That was before I came to work here."

"How interesting. Thank you for the whisky," Anthony said, and glancing at James, raised his glass to celebrate the confirmation of their information. As they were relaxing in silence, their host Timothy Blackwood strode in with a broad smile and an extended hand for Anthony. "Hello sir, welcome to Club 17. And Lieutenant Colonel Horn. I am so delighted that you want to join our ranks. It's an honour gentlemen, a genuine honour." He was quite tall and a very presentable young man, about the age of Butterworth.

"Kind of you to say," Anthony told him.

"I hope I haven't kept you waiting."

"Not at all. James and I were just savouring this marvellous whisky."

"Splendid, I think I'll join you. Thornaby, I'll have a glass of whisky as well."

"Right you are, sir"

"Gentlemen, please sit. So, what do you think of the place?"

Anthony had looked up Blackwood's pedigree and found that he came from good country stock up in the Lake District, the second son of Sir Daniel Blackwood. "From what we have seen of it so far, Tim, this is absolutely top drawer," he said. "What clever magic did you ever employ to find it?"

"Magic indeed. A plum if there ever was one, yes? It belonged to a good friend, a gift from his father upon finishing at Eaton. Bart turned it into our private club straight away and asked us all to join him."

"Would that benefactor have been Hollister Butterworth?" James asked.

"It was. You read up on us, didn't you? How very keen you are, jolly good. To be honest, the location couldn't have been better. None of us could have imagined such good fortune."

"All?" asked Anthony. "Is there a core group at the head of this membership?"

"There was," he said, his voice immediately lost its air of excitement, "The Enlightened Twelve we called ourselves. Rather cheeky of us, wasn't it? Turned out we weren't enlightened at all. Just silly boys playing at being soldiers. But Africa knocked it out of us all, I suppose we came home as the chastened ten."

"Hard luck."

"Yes. We don't talk about those times much anymore."

Anthony placed his hand on Tim's shoulder and said quietly, "We all left friends behind."

"Oh, I know that, but the loss stays with you, doesn't it?"

"It does. I am sorry, old boy."

"Thanks awfully. But then, Bart wandered in as if nothing had happened, the same miserable old chap as always.

"It was utterly amazing, right out of the blue. He said he was in hospital in Jo-burg, lost his memory completely, didn't know who he was. What had he been doing all this time we asked? He said he came to his senses one day and found himself in business with some Dutchmen in Amsterdam, of all places."

"You're joking?" Anthony said. James found the direction of their conversation very enlightening and thought it best to just let the two of them chat.

"Not at all. He would stay in London for a few days, slept in the rooms here in the club, then back to the continent to do business. He'd be gone for months at a time."

"Really, and what sort of business was he doing?"

"You know, that was a question we used to ask him, but he never said. We guessed that it might be import export or some such thing. He didn't deny it, so we just assumed that we'd guessed it. But when he... when he died we didn't hear a word from his people in Amsterdam."

"Odd, don't you think?"

"To be sure. I thought something awful must have happened over there, and that must have been the reason why he did it."

"Did it?" Anthony asked, as if he didn't know.

"Killed himself, put a bullet through his head upstairs in the Collections Room."

"That was a dreadful thing to do.

"Yes, I couldn't agree more. None of us saw it coming. He was in his usual high spirits that morning. We had lunch and made plans to do a bit of a pub crawl that evening. I'm at a loss, frankly."

"You mentioned that you returned short by two," James said. "Who was the second man?

"That was Arthur. Arthur Shaw. He was wounded as well, took a bullet to the head. Don't know how he survived really, but the Boer took him into care and apparently looked after him until he died."

"You didn't mention that Bart Butterworth was wounded."

"Didn't I? Yes, caught one in the shoulder. He was attended to by one of ours, but then it got infected, and they took him away. We all thought it strange that they did that for him, while there were others whose wounds became infected, or they got sick, and the Boers simply left them to die."

Just then another member burst into the room raising his voice, "Blackwood there you are! I've been looking all over the place for you. We need a fourth for bridge."

"No can do chum, I'm lunching with a couple of old friends from Salisbury."

"Oh gawd, that horrible place? Well, how positively dreadful." Focusing his glib jabber on James, he asked, "Is Timmy putting you up for membership then?"

"You know perfectly well that I am, Will."

He bowed with dramatic flourish. "Then, welcome gentlemen, and I am sure you will find our digs exceed anything, and everything that the Salisbury Mess had on offer." He reached out his hand. "I'm William Jenkins."

"James Horn, and my friend, Anthony Hillman."

"A pleasure James, Tony," he said, with a most unwelcome familiarity.

Tim attempted to regain control of the little gathering. "William, we were just about to go through for lunch, would you care to join us and chat up the club a little?"

"Love to, dear boy, but the gang is hankering to head out for lunch. I've come down to ask you to come along."

"Well, you'll just have to dash off without me, I'm afraid."

"Of course, quite right. Say, Tim, old bean, I hate to be a bore, but it would be a hell of a lot easier on yours truly if you could break the sad news to them."

"Oh really, must I?"

"It's for the good of the team, Tim. Gentlemen, I promise this won't take long."

"Gosh, sorry fellows, through thick and thin, as they say. I'll just pop upstairs and be back in a jiff. In the meantime, please enjoy the whisky."

"Tim," William urged from the doorway and James was clearly angered by the interruption. "Do come on dear boy, they are waiting!" His annoyance passed quickly as they listened to what was said outside the room. Jenkins said, "I couldn't help overhearing you talking about Bart and Arthur."

"What about it?"

"Good heavens Tim, we all agreed not to discuss them with outsiders."

"I know that, but my friends are joining the club surely they…" At that point their conversation faded as they hurried up the stairs, leaving James and Anthony wondering if it was guilt that led to that decision. What role might the gang have played in the murder?

Returning to their chairs James said, "Nice job with our host, by the way, Anthony. You managed to get quite a bit out of him."

"He was like that in Rhodesia, a real chatterbox. All I had to do was wind him up and he'd talk for hours."

James laughed quietly then, after having a sip he said, I should like to get a look at the Collections Room. I need to get a sense of the place, how the killer must have stood, etcetera."

"I'll see to it that Tim puts it on the tour." They chatted for some time, wondering silently what had happened to Tim.

The sound of a man running downstairs caught their attention halting their conversation.

A moment later Sgt. Fry rushed into the room breathless and agitated. Gentleman, you must come, quickly!"

"What the devil is going on?" James demanded.

"Something dreadful has happened to Mr. Blackwood!"

"Good Lord man, calm yourself," James demanded. "Now what are you going on about?"

"It's Tim Blackwood... He's dead, sir."

"Dead? But he..." They sped across the room to the door, passing Fry as he ran.

"How did it happen?" Anthony asked, as he went by.

"He just hanged himself," Fry said.

James came to a screeching halt at the doorway and stopped Fry in his tracks.

"What do you mean he hanged himself? That's ridiculous! He was just here a moment ago. He wouldn't have simply gone upstairs to hang himself."

"All I know, sir,. is I was just passing the men's lounge when I heard a thud, I thought a bench had toppled over, so I went in to see what and happened, and-and... Well, there he was."

"Were you certain that he was dead?"

"There was no doubt about it, sir."

"Damn. Have you called the police?"

"No, sir. I came to alert you first."

"Alright, do that right now, and see to it that no one leaves the building until they get here. Hillman and I will go up and attend to Blackwood."

"Yes, sir." He stood back. "Sir?"

"Yes, Fry what is it?"

"I can't believe that he would do such a thing. He was so cheerful this morning," the old man said, then he trotted off to the telephone.

"Fry!" James called after him."

"Sir?"

"Where is the men's lounge?"

"Oh, right. Up the stairs, second-floor, first door on the right."

"Good, now go ahead and make that call."

"Yes sir."

Sensing a conspiracy, James nudged Anthony's arm, saying, "Are you sensing a pattern?"

"I am. That was exactly what Blackwood had said about Butterworth."

"Exactly." James checked the time as the pair made their way to the stairs. It was nearly half past one. They took the steps two at a time, pushed on the lounge door, entered, and Anthony pushed a chair against the door so they wouldn't be disturbed.

The young man hung by a cord suspended from a wall fixture. His body was facing to the wall. The chair from which he stepped, lay on its front across the floor, as if he had given it a good kick as he stepped off.

"Do you find it odd that he is facing the wall?" asked James.

"He should be facing outward I should think."

"Exactly what I was thinking."

James projected a thought, "A suggestion of shame perhaps?"

"I'm not sure what to think now. He didn't give me the impression of being ashamed of anything."

"I agree. Perhaps that idea of shame was the killer's intention."

Anthony studied his friend. "So, you think this was a murder as well?"

"I am certain of it. Fry said he heard a thump and came in to investigate. Unless Blackwood's neck snapped the moment he stepped off the chair it would have taken some time to strangle to death. I would expect there would also be some thrashing about."

"Fry didn't say anything about that sort of thing."

"Yes, and I'd like to know why."

Perhaps James was speaking so softly that Anthony didn't hear him. "I wonder if what Jenkins was discussing with him led to this."

"Are you suggesting that this might indeed be suicide, Anthony?

"No, not at all. But perhaps the culmination of their argument put the young fellow here like this."

"I wonder what time the other members left for lunch."

"I think we should ask Fry, don't you?" said Anthony.

"I do."

Before they left the room, Anthony checked his pockets for anything that might be a clue as to what happened. "Perhaps there was something that the killer planted in him after the deed was done." After a careful search, making sure he didn't disturb the body too much, he said, "No joy there." He looked down to the floor. "James, have a look there."

A small amount of blood had pooled beneath his body. "Where do you suppose that came from?"

Anthony found the source "It seems to be dripping from his wrists." Anthony touched the blood on the floor. "It hasn't fully coagulated. Let's have a look up here."

He pushed up the sleeve of his coat and found the shirt sleeve soaked with blood. Moving it up he sucked in his breath in surprise. "James, have a look at this."

"My goodness. Well, that certainly confirms it."

The traitor's Brand had been cut into his arm, presumably with a pen knife. "Judging from the amount of blood on the floor I'd say the cuts were made after he died,' Anthony said.

James said, "And Fry's story is a complete fabrication."

"His second lie."

"To be sure. I shouldn't think one could fire a shot in this building without it being heard," James answered thoughtfully. "The question now is, could he be our killer?"

"I hardly think he could overpower Tim and string him up like that."

"I agree. I wonder if there is another door into this room. Let's have a..." At that moment, someone pushed on the door handle moving the chair out of the way. "Were we expecting visitors?" Anthony's grave expression turned into a wry smile.

"Police! Open up!"

"Coming constable." Anthony strode over and slid the chair out of the way.

The first constable entered angrily. "Why was this door blocked!"

"Gosh constable, I was about to ask myself the same question."

"Go on, get out of it and stand over there," the policeman growled, and just as they crossed the hall Sergeant Willows arrived at the top of the stairs and immediately spotted James. His expression showed he was less than thrilled to him. "Allo, allo, allo! What the 'ell are you doing 'ere?" he bellowed. "And who is this other joker?"

"DS Willows," James said, with a light happy voice and a smile, "what an unpleasant surprise. We dropped in for lunch and discovered that out host had inexplicably died"

"Well, that's your story is it?" he said, looking dubious. "Looks to me more like you lot showed up for a bit of a chin wag and your host run off and hanged his self. Go on then, tell me that's not what happened."

"If I must," James replied, smoothly. "But first Anthony, may I introduce the illustrious DS Willows."

"Don't play your games with me, Mr. Horn. I got you pegged. What are you two doing here in the first place?"

"In truth, we were invited to lunch with that poor fellow there."

"So, you wasn't having a larf at my expense?"

"Sadly, no. And, as you can see, due to circumstances beyond our control our lunch has been cancelled. So, if you don't mind, we shall take our leave."

"You do nothin' of the kind. You was in there with the deceased, weren't ya?"

"We were, but as you can see we did not disturb anything."

"Really?"

Anthony added, "Not a hair on his head, or a flake of dandruff on his shoulder. We thought to keep the door locked to protect the integrity of the crime scene." They both smiled to reinforce their collective innocence.

"You're having me on ain't ya. Well, I may not be as stupid as I look."

"Oh God, I should hope not," James said.

"Right... er, what did you mean by that?"

"Not a thing DS Willows, nothing at all. So, if you don't mind, we will be on our way."

It took a moment, but then the meaning of James' comment donned on him. "Here what did you say?"

"I was just saying that we should leave now so as to allow you to carry on with your important work."

"Too right you are, but don't leave the building till I've had a word with you about this lot."

"Oh, we wouldn't dream of it, DS Willows."

Sergeant Fry was standing in the doorway. "And who the hell might you be?" Willows asked.

"Don't you remember me, DS Willows? I'm Sergeant Fry, I met you downstairs."

"Of course, I remember you," he said.

"Fry, after you've had a chance to tell what you know to DS Willows, we should like to have a word with you in the Collections Room if we may."

His head swivelled sharply in their direction, a sure indication that he knew he'd been caught out in a lie. He was barely holding it together as he said, "I'll be with you as soon as I can gentlemen."

Placing his hand on Anthony's arm, James stopped him from going after Fry. "Our chance will come in due time," he said, and they stayed at the top of the stairs to listen to the conversation between Fry and Willows. Disappointingly, Willows began with orders rather than questions.

"I want you to gather all the members together in one room so that I can talk to them."

"I'm sorry but all of the members have already left the building, Detective." That instantly got the detective's back up.

"I thought I told you on the telephone to keep everyone here."

"And I would have done just like you said, Detective Sergeant, but the members left the building just before one o'clock. That was before poor Mr. Blackwood done himself."

"Well alright then, I want to talk to whoever is left."

"Of course, that would be the orderly, the cook and his assistants in the kitchen, then there's Lieutenant Colonel Horn, Major Hillman, and myself."

"Alright, alright, you do go on, don't ya? So, what you're telling me, is that there were no members in the club at the time that this man hanged himself?"

"Yes, that would be correct, Detective Sergeant."

"Constable, get the names of the members from this man, then round up a few of the boys and haul them in for questioning."

"Got it."

Fry piped up, "I am afraid that would be quite impossible, Detective Sergeant. I have no idea where they might have gone."

"You are beginning to try my patience Mr. Fry. I'll be needing their addresses, and we'll be tracking 'em down." DC Vance entered the room to take photographs of the scene, including the blood on the floor. When Willows saw that he went out to call the gentlemen back and found them waiting patiently at the stairs.

"What are you two doing hanging about for?"

James had been trying to look as disinterested as possible when he said, "We thought you might like to ask us some questions at some point."

"Uh... Well, as it 'appens, I wouldn't mind 'aving a chat you two. So, if your Lordships wouldn't mind making your way back in 'ere." They joined the other officers around the body, still hanging from the light fixture. "Right, what can you tell me about this blood on the floor?"

"Perhaps he cut himself while hanging," Anthony offered.

"This is not time for jokes, Mr. Hillman. By the look of you, I 'ave a feeling you know somping, so let's have it."

"Alright then, I suggest you follow the track of the blood up to his arm."

"Go on then," he said to the constable.

He did so and found the two arrows carved into the flesh. "Now why would the man do that to his self?"

While James was focused on Sergeant Fry, Anthony said, "Our conjecture was that he didn't."

"Didn't what?"

"Didn't carve that on his wrist. The tiny amount of bleeding would indicate that the mark was cut some minutes after his death."

Fry paled instantly and began heading for the door.

"And where might you be going?" Willows asked."

"I just thought I'd go fetch the rest of my staff for you."

"I 'ave a constable doing that, thank you very much. Now, what do you know about this cutting business?"

"Nothing at all, DS Willows. I just came in here when I heard a noise and I found him like that."

"Did you now?" He walked over to Fry and began poking him in the chest with a pudgy finger. "How would you like to turn out your pockets for me?"

"Really, do you think that's necessary? I mean it's not as if I am a suspect, is it?"

"Humour me, Mr. Fry." He did as he was asked with very little to show for it. A packet of cigarettes, a flint lighter, some coins, a fountain pen, a note pad, and a full set of keys. "Where is your pen knife?"

"I don't have one. This is the twentieth century after all, and as you can see I use a fountain pen like everybody else."

"Harrumph," Willows grunted. "Alright. Would I be wasting my time if I asked you two gents to turn out your pockets?"

"You would find that we both carry revolvers, bill folds, keys and handkerchiefs, no knives."

"Handguns?"

"Come now DS Willows, he was hanged, not shot."

"Aright constable, cut him down and turn out his pockets, let's see if there was anything to tell us what was on his mind before he tossed it in."

James' curiosity got the better of him. "Tell me, are you still thinking that this is a case of suicide, Willows?"

"Mind your own business."

"I would hope that given enough time you will come to appreciate that it is quite impossible to use a knife to mutilate your arm after you are dead."

"Go on, get out of here."

"Thank you. If we may borrow Sergeant Fry for a moment."

"What for? Never mind, yeah, go on with you."

"Sergeant?"

"Uh..." It was clear that he wasn't prepared to go with them willingly.

James took his arm at the elbow. "Are you coming, Fry?"

"Yes Colonel. But if I may, I'd like to answer the call first. There's another toilet in my flat. I'll just go there, won't be a minute. Just through there is the Collections Room, we can talk there."

"Fry, I think you should really come with us while you have a chance."

Fry shook loose of James' grip and made a run for it to the back stairs. Anthony was quick on his heels with James following. a moment later the constables in the lounge came out in time to see him vanish down the servant's hall.

James found Anthony on the landing looking lost. "Where is he?"

"I don't know. I was right behind him and when I turned the corner he was gone."

"Here, what are you two up to now?"

Anthony replied, "Well, to be honest, I think our friend Sgt. Fry had something to do with this and has taken off."

DS Willows was right on the constable's heels and heard Anthony. He shouted back, "Oi, you lot, the old bugger's done a runner! Search the building top to bottom and be quick about it."

"Is he a suspect?"

"Yeah, something like that," Willows said.

The constables scrambled into action, one going up and the other three down the front and back stairs.

"What now?" Anthony asked.

"We were going to the Collections Room."

The collection was in a large room that spanned the width of the building. There were glass front cabinets on three sides and illustrations and paintings on the walls above of scenes from Africa.

One caught Anthony's eye and he was immediately drawn to it. "James, have a look at this."

"What have you got there? I say, haven't I seen that somewhere before?"

"Quite possibly. See the marks of the staples? It's an illustration taken right out of the magazine. It's by an American artist, Richard Caton Woodville. He has drawn the Battle of Tweedosch. Now why would it be displayed so prominently in this room?"

The Battle of Tweedosch, by Richard Caton Woodville Jan 1, 1902.

During the last phase of the war, General De La Rey raided a British garrison and made off with supplies and weapons. Enraged by the sheer audacity of the attack, General Lord Metheun led a column down to Tweebosch with as much speed as he could manage in order to catch the Boer leader. Many of the soldiers in his column were new recruits, untested in battle. And as they raced through Little Harts River, they were unaware that the Boer knew they were coming and had been lying in wait.

De La Rey's men came around them and caught them from behind in an ambush. Metheun's force scattered in panic. The General was among the wounded, and 600 men were captured. The loss was hugely embarrassing for the British Army.

"At least two of Club 17's members that we know of were in that battle. Perhaps it's there to honour them."

"Or to remind them of their failure," James suggested.

Behind the glass doors was a display of weaponry collected from every conflict during the building of the British Empire. Lances, swords, shields spears and guns of all descriptions, made a colourful and impressive display. Each piece was fixed on small brass hooks against a background of green satin.

"And look there," Anthony said. "A missing piece, and I'd say by that dark silhouette where the fabric had been shielded from the sunlight, it was our murder weapon."

"By its shape," James noted, "I'd say it was a Webley which was now in the hands of the curators at the Scotland Yard Museum."

Beneath the cabinets were rows of drawers labelled to indicate what lay inside. More guns, knives, and other relics along with maps from the Boer wars, the Raj, and the Crimean.

The wing-back chair in which Butterworth had died, had been cleaned. The woodwork of the cabinet across the room, scarred by the bullet, had been temporarily covered over with brown wax while they waited for the cabinet maker to repair the damage. Standing behind the chair, James took aim with his finger imagining where the victim sat and how he would have to pose in order to fit the police photographs of the scene. The men paid close attention to the trajectory, confirming that Butterworth had been facing the right side, towards Buckingham Palace when he was shot.

"This would be so much easier with Fry here."

"Do you think he is our killer?" Anthony asked.

"One must never count a man out when it comes to this sort of cowardly foul play, so it certainly is possible, but I don't think so. Timothy would have been more than a match for him without a weapon. By the way he behaved after we questioned him about the hanging suggested to me that he was a party to it."

"You think so?"

"Yes, perhaps to lure him into a trap. That, I think would be more in character for the man."

They returned to the hall as Willows was exiting the men's lounge. "I say, Willows, have your men found Sergeant Fry?"

"No, the man vanished."

"Did he leave the building?"

"I have men posted front an' back, if 'e did try to leave my men would have seen 'im."

"I see." James said, then he recalled something he meant to check when the first constable interrupted them. Are you finished with that room?"

"Yeah, you want back in there?"

"We do as a matter of fact."

"What for?"

"I have a niggling feeling that we may have missed something. Would you mind letting us have a peek?"

The superintendent had called Willows out for being so dismissive of Colonel Horn and was not about to repeat the offense.

"I suppose not."

"Thank you."

Once inside Anthony asked quietly, "Have we actually forgotten something?"

To that James replied even more quietly. "Yes, I'm thinking there might be a second way of entering this room."

"It would have to be a secret passage then, because I didn't see another door."

"That was just what I was thinking."

"The only place it might be, would be behind that towel rack."

"Then why don't you give the towel rack a bit of a push?" James said encouragingly.

Anthony did with no success. He tried rotating the rack from the right side and then the left, again with no success. On his fourth attempt, he tried to slip it sideways to the left. "No." Then to the right and that was the movement that did the trick. To Anthony's surprise, the wall pushed back then swung out of the way. "By Jove, how did you think of that?"

"It just came to me." Beyond the secret door was a narrow passage that led to a steep staircase. James called out, "I say, DS Willows, I think you should come and have a look at this."

"Yes, what is it?" The large man lumbered in and looked over James' shoulder. "Upon my word! Who would have thought a building like this would have a hidden doorway? Where does it lead?"

"I have no idea. Perhaps you should explore it and find out."

"It'll be a tight squeeze, but I think I will."

And with the aid of a torch he tread carefully into the dark.

"As to your earlier question Anthony, I think that my final thought was the correct one. Someone was in here waiting for Fry to lead the victim in. I suspect the coroner will discover a lump on Timothy's head. Once rendered unconscious, Fry helped the killer set the scene and then came for us to confirm his lie. I would dearly love to have a conversation with that phantom if they can take him alive."

"You sound as if you are in some doubt about that."

"To be honest, I am." A torchlight lit up the passageway announcing Willows' return. "What did you discover down there?"

"The killer was in the building the whole time. I found Mr. Fry in the cellar. His throat's been cut. We now 'ave a double murder on our hands gentlemen."

"There is nothing more we can do here, Anthony. I think we should return to Warwick Square."

Mrs. Findley greeted them at the door. "My word gentlemen, aren't you are a pair of clouds on a sunny day."

Anthony said, "It was not a successful outing I'm afraid, Mrs. Findley." After James went into his study and closed the door, Anthony gave her a short briefing on what transpired. He acknowledged her look of concern with a sad smile. "He is taking it rather hard. Perhaps if we hadn't gone there to question him Timothy would still be alive."

"You can't know that. What if the killer had already been there waiting for him? The result would have been the same had you gone or not."

"You may be right?"

"Of course I am," she said, satisfied that she had made a contribution. "You two gentlemen have to remember that the world doesn't begin and end with you.

"For good or for bad, it just ticks along as it has always done."

"How very wise."

"I have my moments, don't I." She headed back to her kitchen, but before she disappeared, she said, "I've prepared a light tea for you if you're hungry."

"I couldn't eat a bite to be honest."

"That's fine, dear. I'll just go along and see if his Lordship is hungry."

Before she made her way down the hall, James opened his door and said, "I am writing a note to Miss Butterworth detailing what we have discovered to this point. It isn't much more than bad news I'm afraid. If you have anything to add Anthony, it's on my desk. I need to clear my head. Perhaps a walk will help."

"Oh, I was just going to ask you if you'd like some tea."

"Thank you, no."

"Shall I wait tea until you return?"

"I shouldn't bother, Mrs. Findley."

Needing to be alone, James strolled down to the Thames and when he met the wall, turned north and walked on aimlessly. So deep in thought was he that without noticing where he was he found himself at the entrance of Spring Gardens, near the back door of the Scotland Yard. Had he planned to bump into Henry Dobbs, his timing could not have been better.

"James, what the devil are you doing here?"

"Henry, I… Hello, I seem to have drifted into your path. How extraordinary."

"Oh, my old chum, if you were trying to convince me that this was a meeting of unwitting coincidence, then you will have to do better than that. What's on your mind?"

"You have no doubt heard of the murders at 17 Catherine Place."

"I have. A shocking situation."

"To be honest, Henry, this mystery has caused me to be concerned for the safety of all the other members of Club 17. By the way, Willows seems to have come around. What did you say to the man?"

"I suggested he might get fitted out for a blue uniform if he didn't smarten up!" James chuckled. "He said that this Blackwood chap was murdered while you were there to lunch with him?"

"It is true. He left us to talk with some other members and while we waited for his return we were informed by the accomplice that Timothy Blackwood had killed himself."

"Good heavens! Are you sure of this?"

"The proof was in the second murder, when the killer turned on his accomplice and slit his throat. The man is a monster."

"Willows performed well, did he?"

"The hippopotamus cannot change his way over night, Henry. But I will admit that he has some qualities worth cultivating. Willows found the secret passageway and followed it to the body in the cellar. The mark of two arrows that was on the gravestone was cut into the arms of both victims."

"So, we are dealing with a homicidal maniac."

"I have no doubt. But what puzzles me is why he waited eighteen months to strike again?"

"Perhaps changing circumstances have affected his motivation."

"Anthony quipped about it having something to do with the nonsense in Serbia..."

"Yes, precisely."

"And I would be inclined to agree, but for the fact that the mark relates to something that happened in South Africa. Do you recall the Battle of Tweebosch?"

"Vaguely."

"At least two of the club members were there and were captured along with Lord Metheun. It is quite possible that the Traitor's Brand could be directly linked to that disaster."

"Is that what you are calling it now?"

"I believe that it has become a symbol of cowardice and treason. What I would like to know now is could the changing circumstances in Europe link them?"

"I can't answer that for you, James."

"I wonder if anyone can. The significance must relate to some experience those men shared in the Boer's prison camp, and that experience has regained its importance in some way."

"Willows posited that the man was a coward and a deserter."

"Obviously, that is how I read it. Now there seems to be a second, more sinister interpretation."

"What the devil could that be?"

"Your guess is as good as mine. Hence the reason for my walk this evening.

"I'll put my people on it right away."

"Thank you."

"James, if you are able to divine the answer, do remember to share it with your friend at the Yard?"

"I will, Henry. I promise."

After walking for another ten minutes, James realised that he was more tired than he had given credit and hailed a cab. "Number 5 Warwick Square?"

"Right you are, governor."

*****

CHAPTER ~ 5

HYDE PARK ROSE GARDEN

A man rang up James the following day and though he would not give his name, he said that he had seen James at Club 17 and it was urgent that they talk. As James had seen a number of people there, he had no idea who or how many other people might have seen him. "We are talking now, so tell me what it is that you want?"

"Not on the phone. They can't be trusted."

"I see. Alright, but before I agree to meet with you, I must know your name."

"Just think of me as a friend."

"The kind of friend who wrote that letter to Miss Butterworth?"

"The very same."

"Well friend, that is not good enough. Obviously, you need something from me and the price is your name. So, do you want to meet or not?" James asked.

"I know the murderer, and I know why he did it."

"You don't trust the telephones? Well, I don't trust you. Your name. Last chance before I hang up."

"Since you insist…" His comment was delivered snidely.

"Damn. I am hanging up now."

"No wait!"

"Then stop messing about!"

"It's William Jenkins. Please, I must see you."

"Alright," James paused, wondering if this was going to be a waste of time. "When and where?"

"Tonight, the Hyde Park Rose Garden, nine o'clock. If you come, then I will tell you everything." With that said, the line was disengaged.

For the rest of the day, he pondered whether this meeting was folly. At best, it would be a wasted evening, at worst it could be a trap. It wasn't until the end of dinner that he made his decision to go at all.

"And…" Prompted Anthony.

"Yes, and I'm going in alone."

"Ridiculous, most likely it's a trap," Anthony said. James remained resolute. "Alright, like it or not, I am following you. I will be nearby, but out of sight."

"That would be much appreciated. Thank you."

He wore the quick draw shoulder holster made for him in Calcutta to carry his small revolver, which he carried for just this sort of situation.

Even in summer, the chill of London nights always reminded him of the frigid nights on the African veldt. Leaving the house in his camel hair overcoat, leather gloves, and Homburg he stepped into the cab. "Drop me off at the Rose Garden at Hyde Park." With caution and some trepidation, he made his way warily to the appointed meeting place.

By the light of the moon, he saw the shadowy figure of a man standing by the Huntress Fountain.

An uncertain voice called out, "Lieutenant Colonel Horn, is that you, sir?"

"The same." There was certainly something familiar about him, but the voice was not the one he heard on the phone, the man who had invited him. "And would you be William Jenkins?"

"Yes. Thank God it's you. When you called and told me to come here I didn't know what to think. Is it about Tim. God what a terrible mess this is."

"Mr. Jenkins, I did not call you. I was summoned here to be told the identity of our killer. So, am I to believe that would be you?"

"No! Why on Earth would I do that? Tim was my friend."

"It has been known to happen. Nevertheless, I'll accept your statement as fact for the moment. And whilst we are dispensing facts, the police took a rather dim view of you and your chums leaving the club. They were certain that you were involved in some way."

"We weren't, not at all. We simply decided to go out to lunch, that was why I interrupted you and we left right after that. I wanted Tim to join us, but he was committed to lunch with you. It was all quite amicable I assure you. He told us to go ahead and have fun. God, this is terrible. Poor Tim. I can't understand why anyone would do such a thing."

"Nor can I. Alright, I believe you. Now I want you to come with me," James said, as he drew his revolver.

"Oh my God, you're not going to shoot me, are you?"

"Don't talk rot man, of course not. However, there is an exceptionally good chance that we have been coaxed here by someone who does. Quickly now."

Jenkins was behaving stoically as they left the park and walked briskly out onto the street. James decided to ask his question while he had the chance. "How well did you know Bart Butterworth?"

"We went through Eton together and a year at Cambridge reading English literature. As a matter of fact, we all did, the Enlightened Twelve. It was a rather silly thing really. We all thought we were so brilliant that we formed the club. Then when Bart's father gave him the house..."

"On Catherine Place?"

"Yes, he sort of made the club official with Club 17."

"I see." They walked along and were beginning to feel safe in each other's company.

"Why are you so curious about Bart Butterworth?"

"I noticed the odd inscription on his gravestone and became very curious about why someone would have had that strange epitaph engraved on it."

"I never saw it, don't like cemeteries or funerals."

"How interesting. I thought it might have been a memorial contributed by one of his friends."

"I assure you; it did not come from any of us. We were on the outs with him long before his suicide. When he appeared out of the blue like that he seemed like a completely different person. He was rude, irrational and temperamental."

"I see."

"It was no wonder he did himself in."

"In point of fact, he didn't. He was murdered just as Tim was. Sgt. Fry was a part of it as well."

"I can't believe it. Did Fry confess?"

"Not in so many words, but his actions were rather convincing. The killer took his life as well."

"This is overwhelming." He walked on in silence for a few steps than asked, "What was written on the stone?"

"It said, 'Brother, Betrothed, Bastard.' Why would he be described as a bastard? I have drawn a complete blank."

"Well, for a start I'd say that if the man wasn't already dead he could have written that nonsense himself."

"An interesting observation, but the question of the word bastard needs an explanation. What do you say to that?"

Beyond their notice a policeman was keeping pace with them, walking silently in the shadows.

"That is easy enough to answer," Jenkins said, becoming more relaxed. "The chap was both an illegitimate child and, as I said, he had a nasty streak. He would lash out cruelly, and sometimes violently without provocation."

"I see. How is it that you know about his illegitimacy?'

"He told us. I mentioned his irrational behaviour, well that was one of the topics of which he seemed to take particular delight. Sometimes he'd claim it was his sister, then say he was only joking, and that he was the bastard. He'd tell anyone who'd listen. It seemed to be a point of pride to him that he found his way into such a wealthy family. He gambled all the time. Well, he had the money didn't he? A seemingly inexhaustible flow of it. He would brag about receiving ten thousand a year. Can you imagine that? The topic grew quite tiresome actually.

"As far as I knew, there was no secret that he possessed that he wouldn't share."

"That paints a very sad picture of a man." James considered his next question carefully. "You said he gambled. On what, exactly?"

"Anything, everything, every chance he got. He was the type of man that would bet on which drop of rain would arrive at the bottom of a windowpane first. It was nauseating the way he threw his money around. I'm not surprised his father didn't leave him the business."

"Is it correct that none of you cared for him?"

"As I said, he was a hard man to care for. Arthur liked him, I suppose."

"Did he talk about his sister at all?"

"Whoa-ho, I should say he did. My goodness, he wouldn't stop talking about her. She stole the business, he said."

Other than the epitaph, James wasn't about to give anything away. "Did she?"

"Did she what?"

"Steal the business."

"As far as he was concerned she did. But she was the one who inherited it, not him. He was livid when they read his father's will. That may have been the turning point for him, when he realised that his father wasn't going to hand the company over to him. He said he'd kill Jennifer. You know, I think he would have, had he known where she was. I believe Jennifer must have been aware of his feelings and saw to it that he took that threat to his grave. Bart thought going to war with the Boer would raise his stock in his father's heart, but that was a gamble that he well and truly lost. His father never forgave him for his needless sacrifice."

"Really?"

"Oh yes, it seemed everything Bart did put him in wrong with the old man. He said his mother was the only one from whom he received any sympathy at all."

"You mean his stepmother."

"There is the funny thing, he never referred to her as his stepmother. Then we were all captured in that terrible ambush. Arthur and he were among the wounded."

"You mentioned that name before. Who is Arthur?"

"That should be, who was Arthur. Well to begin, he was a wonderful chap. His last name was Shaw, Arthur Shaw. You know, I truly miss that man."

"Quite understandable. Please continue."

"Anyway, when the Boer took Lord Metheun away they took hundreds as well, Arthur and Bart among them. We had heard that Metheun was repatriated, which was very unusual to say the least."

"Yes, our side was quite sceptical about the reasons behind that, and it caused quite a fuss."

"I'm glad. There was no mention of anyone else being sent home, so we naturally thought that Arthur and Bart had died. So you can imagine our surprise when some years later Bart showed up very much alive."

"A broken man."

"Yes." He pondered that for a moment. "I suppose it wasn't really his fault. Lots of men lost their minds down there."

"True enough," said James. "That clears up that question nicely, thanks. Tell me about that, the ambush."

"Gosh, what a terrible day that was. As you probably know, De La Ray was waiting for us, we were at Methuen's side when they came at us from behind. We were pushing hard and going too fast to realise what was happening. Methuen was hit three times before he fell. Arthur and Adam..."

"Who is Adam?"

"One of the lads, a good chap as well. They dismounted to see to the general and Arthur took a bullet in the face, Adam was shot in the back. Bart rode to Arthur immediately and was shot off his horse. I saw him lying next to Arthur and thought them both dead.

"When the dust settled, we were surrounded. I was sure the Boer were going to kill us all but instead they took us prisoner. At the time I didn't know which was worse, frankly. They loaded Methuen and the other wounded into our wagons and marched the rest of us south to a prison camp."

"Just out of curiosity, to whom was Bart betrothed?"

"Oh my gosh, it couldn't have been a more tragic story. She was Arthur's sister, Cynthia Shaw. Oh my, she was a lovely, wonderful girl and none of us, including Arthur, could understand what she saw in Bart."

"I gather the engagement was broken off."

"It was indeed. As we understand it, when he convinced Arthur to join up with the rest of us. She couldn't forgive that, and said she never wanted to see him again. I understand that she fled the city."

"Do you know where she went?"

"Haven't a clue. Bart was heartbroken of course and became rather bitter about it. Arthur was able to console him I think, and..."

Before he could finish his thought a shot rang out from behind some trees which instantly ended his life.

James quickly returned fire aiming for the area where he'd seen the muzzle flash, but it was simply an automatic response, the killer was gone.

Dropping to his knee James felt for a pulse. He was gone.

He struck a match and lifted Jenkins' left arm then pushing back his sleeve he looked to see if he bore the mark.

He didn't expect to see one there, but he had to look.

Someone was running towards him. Still kneeling, he crouched down lower as he turned his gun in that direction. He was prepared to fire.

"Hold your fire, James, it's me!" Anthony shouted

"Anthony! Thank goodness you called out. I thought for a moment that you were the shooter."

"I couldn't let you come out here on your own, but I was delayed." He knelt down beside Jenkins and felt for a pulse. "I wasn't much help, was I?"

"You may have frightened the killer off before he shot me as well."

"Who is it?"

"It's Jenkins, the monster shot him through the heart."

When he heard the police whistle coming from the direction in which the killer had fled James relaxed a little. It seemed that the threat was gone and returning the pistol to its holster they both stood up. The policeman's torch suddenly cut through the darkness and James called out to him. "Constable, we are over here, a man has been shot dead." The beam of light flashed in his face, forcing him to shield his eyes. "Yes, right here," he said, calmly.

"I heard two shots, are you armed, sir?" he asked.

"Yes, I returned fire, but the blighter got away got away. I have put it away, so you are safe to come ahead, but there is no need to hurry constable, the man is past any help we could give him."

"Are you injured?"

"No, I'm quite alright."

"Are you armed as well, sir?" he asked Anthony.

"I am, but it too is safely put away."

"Where did the shot come from?"

Pointing to the trees down the path, James said, "He ran off in that direction."

"Blimey. The killer must have run right by me."

"Yes, I think he did."

"And I didn't see a thing." A whistle sounded from down the street. "Splendid, reinforcements," James said. "Whoever he was, his bush craft was excellent. I heard nothing until he fired his gun."

James and Anthony had turned to watch the constables come in from all directions when the first one made a staggering announcement.

"Here, have a gander at this, sir. I found this note in one of his pockets." He shown his torchlight on the paper and read the words printed in large block letters. "And they've drawn a strange diagram on it too. Do you have any idea what this means, sir?"

He showed it to James. YOU ARE NEXT

James' eyes widened. "Why, it is the Traitor's Brand."

"Yes it is. How very interesting. Are you a traitor, sir?"

"Don't be impertinent man." Then to Anthony he said, "Now the question remains, was this note referring to Jenkins or to me?"

During the frenzy of questions fired at them both by the other policemen, James did his best to keep up with it all but he was distracted. Anthony asked the first man to confirm his story. A corporal looked at him suspiciously and asked, "And what man would that be, sir?" James shot his eyes around to find that constable and sure enough, he was gone.

"He agreed when I called it the Traitor's Brand."

"What was that, James?"

"That man was a fraud. He knew I called it the Traitor's Brand."

****

Safely Home

Thankfully, Mrs. Findley slept on when they returned home, tired and depressed. After hanging up his hat and coat James said, "Will you join me in my study? I'd like to talk this over with you if I may."

"Give me a moment would you, I'll be right down," he said, quietly.

"Of course."

Anthony crept up to his rooms to freshen up then hurried down to find James staring into the fire. "Are you alright, James?"

"I am uninjured, but that is the best that I can report."

"This is terribly wearing on you James, I am sorry."

"No need to be Anthony, in for a penny, in for a pound. Oh, forgive me. Please, help yourself to the decanter."

They sat in silence for a while, trying to think of something Jenkins may had said that would lead them to the killer.

Eventually James ended the silence angrily. "What galls me is that his killer was standing right there with us holding that blasted torch!"

"Are you sure it was him?"

"For God's sake, who else could have known that I had named it the Traitor's Brand? He must have heard us talking at Club 17. Why did I not sense that it was our man? How foolish could I have been to let my guard down like that?"

"James, you're not being fair to yourself at all. He was a uniformed policeman shining that torch in your eyes. How could you have known that he was anything but what he appeared to be?"

He was reluctant to forgive himself, but Anthony had made sense.

"Alright, thank you for that." He sat in silence for some minutes before asking, "Where could he have obtained that uniform? Is there now some poor sod lying dead in an alley? This is simply outrageous!"

"James..."

"Who is this man?!"

"James, please keep your voice down, you'll wake..."

There was a soft knock at the door. "Hello in there," Mrs. Findley said, "I couldn't help hearing. Shall I put on the kettle?"

"Sorry to wake you, but that will not be necessary, Mrs. Findley, thank you. Now please, go back to bed."

"Very well. Good night gentlemen."

James snapped back, "Good night!" And having said that, the silence continued until they were sure the housekeeper had gone back to her room.

"I was wrong about him ... about Jenkins I mean," James said, at last. "He was merely trying to convince Timothy to go with them."

"It's a shame that he didn't."

"Yes." More silence followed, as they sipped their whisky, each ruminating on his own thoughts.

Eventually the chill drove Anthony to get up and stoke the fire.

He added more coal. "Is that better?"

James nodded his approval. When he sat down again, Anthony continued. "How did the killer know to follow Jenkins?"

"He didn't have to follow him. He rang him up and invited him to the park using my name."

"How did he manage to involve Fry?"

"I'm sure I don't know," said James.

Anthony reached for the decanter. "A refill?"

Holding out his glass, he said, "Please."

"He could have been tricked into helping the man."

"And his fear may have been doubled by knowing we would eventually accuse him of being a part of."

"But then again James, he displayed a rather easy conscience following the Butterworth murder."

"Perhaps he was telling us the truth about that. Dammit Anthony, frankly I don't know what to think anymore. There are eight bloody men left in that ridiculous club.

"Are they all marked for death as well?"

"What I'm wondering now is, are they all traitors?"

James sat back planting his elbows on the armrests then shot forward again. "Oh my God, that's it!"

"What is it?"

"I must have been half asleep. It is the other way around."

"Kriky, the killer is our traitor?"

"Yes, exactly. I don't know what he stands to gain by this, but I think he is getting rid of witnesses!"

"Then they should all be on their guard."

"We shall deal with that in the morning. And that's it for me, I'm going up to bed." He drained his glass and retired.

****

RETURN TO CLUB 17

There was a brief mention in the newspaper of troubles with the anarchists in Sarajevo in anticipation of the Grand Duke's visit to inspect the troops of the Austro-Hungarian Empire.

Also, the paper devoted two lines to the shooting near Hyde Park and that detectives Horn and Hillman were involved.

The detectives chose that morning to return to Club 17, but unlike their first encounter they were greeted without enthusiasm. "Morning gentlemen, I am Graham Patraquin."

"Mr. Patraquin, I am Lieutenant Colonel..."

"Horn and Major Hillman, yes, I read the morning paper."

"Then you know why we are here."

"Truth be told I was expecting you to turn up and anticipated that you would want to talk to us. I have brought our little group together for you."

"Then perhaps we should come in, don't you think?"

"Oh, how silly of me to have you standing out here. Of course, please." James and Anthony followed the young man up the stairs. "Poor William. Colonel, what is happening? Why were they murdered?"

"Sadly, we have no answers just theories at the moment and the knowledge that you all are at risk."

"So, it is all of us. I was afraid of that."

"And so you should be. That is the one thing that we believe to be fact. Having said that, we are trying as best we can, to discover the reason and expose the culprit." Patraquin opened the door to the card room where the other seven men were seated around two bridge tables. They all stood as James and Anthony entered. "Gentlemen," James said, in greeting.

"Sir," they responded together.

"Please, take your seats."

Patraquin motioned in a circular pattern. "I'll go around the tables shall I? Beginning on your left are captains Huxley and Ogilvy, lieutenants Conroy, Gladstone, Blanchford, and Strand, then finally, majors Attenborough and Overton."

"Thank you for that introduction. From the mention of your ranks, I take it that you are all active once again?"

"There is sure to be a war soon, sir. All the signs point to it," said Lt. Ogilvy.

"Sadly, I have to agree with you Lieutenant. Mr. Patraquin, I didn't get your rank. Have you resumed your commission?"

"I have and was promoted to lieutenant colonel."

"Congratulations."

"Sir, what happened to Jenkins?" Maj. Attenborough asked.

"He and I were tricked into meeting at the Rose Garden last night, each of us thinking that we had come at the other's invitation. Unfortunately, it was a setup, for what purpose other than to murder William Jenkins I can only imagine. Perhaps, as my partner and I seem to be the ones leading the investigation, the killer was taunting us. As soon as we had a chance to talk I realised the danger we were in. We hurried out of the park in the hopes of eluding the killer. Perhaps that was all part of his plan, but who can tell about these things." He paused as the incident replayed in his head.

"Quite right, all you can do is try to anticipate his next move."

"Yes. As we walked down the street the assassin struck from the shadows, killing Jenkins with a shot in the back. I returned fire, but he was gone."

"What happened then?" Conroy asked.

"He was taunting me, approaching me dressed as a police constable. By keeping behind his torchlight, he was able to prevent me from seeing his face, but I'll remember his voice, should I ever chance to hear it again." He took the bit of paper from his pocket. "He presented me with this note, which he claimed to have taken from William's pocket. It says, 'you are next'. His intent was to say it was in his pocket before our meeting, but I doubt that."

"What happened next?"

"The real police arrived and the assassin returned to the shadows once again."

"And now you believe that all the members of the club are at risk," Blanchford said.

Patraquin answered, "No Fred, it's just us that he wants, those of us who were together in the POW camp." That remark gave them all pause.

Anthony spoke next, "I understand that all of you went to lunch the day Timothy Blackwood was murdered?"

"Yes, but how could that have any relevance?" Blanchford asked.

"Don't be so dim, Freddy. He asked because he thought one of us could have been the murderer."

"Oh, of course. Sorry." Embarrassed he looked away.

"As a matter of fact, we did. For obvious reasons, we eliminated Butterworth and Shaw as suspects. Though we had thought that one of you might be our killer, recent events have proven otherwise. Unfortunately, that means he is out to get all of you."

"That gives me the shivers," said Blanchford.

"As it should. One thing puzzles me now. Did any of you arrange for Bart's funeral?" They looked at each other in bewilderment. "That, I take it would be no. But you all attended, yes?"

"There was no notice of a funeral, or a memorial in the papers. When we realised that we had missed it, no one could explain how that could have happened. That whole terrible affair was so strange."

"Indeed, it was. I'm curious about the lost man."

"Shaw, you mean?" Brian Conroy asked.

"Yes, what can you tell us about him?"

"Oh, Arthur was a delightful chap," said Patraquin. "Quite possibly the best of us."

"Hang on there Patraquin," said one man and the others seemed equally offended.

"Oh, do shut up. Don't be such children, you know he was." He walked over to a wall covered in portraits, both paintings and photographs. Pointing to Shaw's picture he said, "We all liked him enormously. This is his portrait, along with the other members who died in the service of King and country. That's Bart there."

"Arthur was a handsome lad," said James, then paused to think.

"Do you recall anyone else in the camp who may have had a grievance with you. Anyone who may have been released earlier, or taken to hospital along with Shaw and Butterworth?"

They looked around at each other and talked it over briefly, but the consensus was that there was no one like that. "For the most part," began Huxley, "we were a tight little group of twelve, then ten of us. There was a time when we expected to get Bart back. But then when he didn't re-join us we just assumed that he had died as well."

"Yes. No one could have been more surprised than we were when he just waltzed in out of the blue like that," said Conroy.

Patraquin continued, "I told him, we'd given him up for dead and then here he was in the pink of health."

"How did he explain it?"

"As a matter of fact, it was quite a story. He said he'd been taken to hospital in Holland. God knows why, but they let General Methuen go home, so we couldn't argue the point. He said he had lost his memory and didn't know who he was. Having nowhere else to go, he settled in Amsterdam and went into business with someone. Then suddenly his memory was restored, and he came home."

"How interesting." Patraquin opened a silver cigarette case and offered James a smoke. "Thank you, no. Do we know who he was working with?"

After lighting his with a silver lighter Patraquin answered, "He didn't give us much by way of details."

"He kept on in business with the fellow, going back and forth for years," added Conroy.

"I see." James pondered the significance of that for a moment then moved on to another topic. "Jenkins mentioned Butterworth's fiancé."

"That would be Cynthia Shaw. Yes, she returned to Scotland," said Patraquin.

"Aha ha. Has anyone had any contact with her since then?"

"No," said Patraquin, "though I had thought of doing so several times. I must admit that I was rather fond of her myself." Most of them nodded their heads. "Yes, most of us were, she was as extraordinary in her way as her brother Arthur was in his." The others concurred.

Struck by the possibility of having lost another witness and possibly a victim, James asked sharply, "You just spoke of her in the past tense. Please tell me that she is still alive."

"Goodness, did I? Forgive me I didn't mean to," he said, looking rather pained at the very thought that she might have died. "Actually, I have no idea. I certainly hope so. I mean, it has been years since I... Well, as far as I know she is alive and well."

*****

Chapter ~ 6

Post Interviews

Looking rumpled and pale, James came down the following morning in a foul mood. Mrs. Findley met him at the bottom of the stairs. "Goodness me. I swear you could haunt a house with that face, Colonel. Can I fix you a nice breakfast?"

"Thank you, no, just coffee please. Is Anthony up?"

"He's in his office I believe. Would you like me to bring your coffee in there?"

"Yes, and would you find something for this beastly headache?" He went straight to the room at the front and knocked before entering. Anthony was at his desk by the window, going over his notes. "What are you up to?"

"I have gone over the group interviews you conducted yesterday, James."

"Good, and ...?" said James, flopping into a chair.

"And I can't find fault with anything they said. They have no idea what is going on." He looked at James, and upon actually seeing him for the first time in his current bedraggled condition, asked, "Couldn't sleep?"

"I could have slept better in a pit of vipers. Honestly Anthony, do you have any idea what is going on here?"

"Didn't you do that one time?"

He stared at his friend incredulously for a few seconds. "Didn't I do what, which one time?"

"Sleep in a pit of vipers."

"Oh, do shut up Anthony, please. Victims are dropping like flies, and I am no mood for your desperate attempts at humour."

"Sorry. I am currently shutting up."

"Wonderful. I haven't heard a word from Miss Butterworth in days and I'm worried sick." Holding his head as if he thought it might fall off. "In the name of Christ!" he cursed softly, "If I don't get some coffee soon I swear..." He sighed heavily and sank back into his chair. "You were saying something about Jenkins."

"Right, having moved on, I was giving some thought to Bartholomew Butterworth's illegitimacy and I..."

A gentle knock interrupted him. "Oh, perhaps that is my coffee come at last. Yes?" As he spoke the housekeeper bumped the door open with her hip.

"Goodness gracious me," Mrs. Findley said gleefully, as she brought in the tray with coffee and headache powders, "have I come just in time to hear some awful gossip?"

James spoke to her with unaccustomed sharpness, "That, my good woman is none of your concern."

"Well, my word," she said indignantly, "listen to Mr. Grumpy. What's put him in such a nasty temper?"

"Apparently, he misses sleeping in a pit of vipers."

"Anthony, what did I just say about your attempts at humour?"

"I do beg your pardon," then whispering to Mrs. Findley he said, "He has been expecting a call from Miss Butterworth, Mrs. Findley, which sadly has not yet come."

"Oh. I am sorry."

"Are you?" snapped James, as he leaped out of his chair. "Are you really?"

Stepping out of his way, she said, "I don't know, to be honest. Should I be?"

"Oh, dear God, spare me."

"Here, why don't you take a seat and calm down before you cause yourself an injury? I've got something for your head..."

"It's about bloody time too."

"... and here is your coffee. And I'm not accustomed to being spoken to like that, your Lordship. I've only got two hands you know."

"I'm sorry, Mrs. Findley," he said holding his head. James collapsed into the chair again. "I don't know what has come over me."

"Well then, thank you for the apology m'lord. Here you are, Major Hillman. I thought you might want some coffee too, so I brought an extra cup."

"Very kind, thank you Mrs. Findley."

Feeling quite guilty, James said, "Yes many thanks, and please forgive my outburst." He then returned to the question they had been discussing before she walked in. "Now Anthony, you were mentioning Butterworth's illegitimacy?"

"Oh right, it was after you told me what Will Jenkins said about Butterworth's origins. Fair warning, all I have at this point is based mostly on an assumption which..."

"Oh, I do love those baseless assumptions."

"Good grief, Mrs. Findley, must you? And why the devil are you still here?"

"I was just..."

"Don't just, do leave, please."

"Your Lordship, you are a cruel and heartless man."

"Hold on there." James looked to her with a raised eyebrow while ominously gripping the arms of his chair.

"What are you going on about Mrs. Findley?" Anthony asked.

"I was just cleaning up his study the other day, when I discovered his secret, that's what I'm going on about. Why would he hide something like this from us?"

"Hide what from us?"

She remained tight lipped, so he was tempted to plead with her, but then resisted the urge.

"Never mind the woman, Anthony, I would just like to have my coffee in peace."

"Why didn't we know that you were an Earl?"

Anthony was stunned. "Is that true? Are you actually an Earl?"

"If you paid any attention, you would have known that after my brother Hugh died; I inherited the title. But as I don't intend to use it, there is no need for anyone else to bother with it either."

Mrs. Findley explained, "He is Lord Horn, III Earl of Reedmont, that's what he is."

"It was never a secret," said James calmly, "and I would be happy as a clam to never hear of it again. Now please may I have my coffee and then perhaps we can get back to work."

"Oh no you don't. By rights it is my title too."

"I beg your pardon?"

"I want to be known as the Housekeeper to the III Earl of Reedmont. I have to uphold my position in the community in which I live, same as you."

"Fine, I grant you the title of Housekeeper to the Earl. But keep in mind Mrs. Findley, the less said about it the better."

"If you say so, and very kind of you, I'm sure," she said, without meaning a word of it.

"And stop snooping in my study, it's not a bloody lending library you know."

"Yes your Lordship. If my George was still with us, I wouldn't have to put up with your temper."

"Oh Lord, how I wish that Sergeant Findley were still with us, so he could take you off my hands. Now, will you please leave and let us get back to work?!"

She snatched up the coffee tray in a huff and was about to withdraw with it.

"Wait! Leave the tray if you don't mind," he said. "You can pick it up later." She slammed it back down on the table and left, without closing the door behind her. James got up and closed the door quietly. "Peace at last." Instead of returning to his chair he walked over to the window, and said, "Please, continue."

"Right, assuming that Mr. Butterworth Sr. had a mistress, and my guess would be that she was Henrietta Langdon of Oxford."

"Yes, that makes sense, hence the second Mrs. Butterworth."

"Exactly. Drawing license from that, I would suggest that Hollister Butterworth discovered his lovely Henrietta was unfortunately with child, a situation that, under normal circumstances, would have caused some considerable awkwardness in the Butterworth household. But as it happened, fortune smiled upon the mischievous couple, as Mrs. Butterworth had also become pregnant at about the same time."

"Perhaps it's the headache, but I fail to see how concurrent pregnancies could possibly be viewed as a case of good fortune."

"True, unless viewed in this way. Let me suggest that Hollister Butterworth no longer held tender feelings for his wife Sandra and saw this as an opportunity to have her gone."

"Are you suggesting that he murdered his wife?"

"No... Well, allow me to amend that by saying perhaps he did in a way. Remember that this is all postulations. I'm not saying that he committed murder."

"Quite right too."

"But, what if he simply failed to help her survive the trauma of a difficult childbirth. That would not be murder, would it?"

"That would be diabolical. Go on."

"Things progress as things often do," Anthony said, warming to his theory, "and nine months later, Hollister decides to move down to London. It is a difficult trip and Sandra is feeling poorly."

"I'm beginning to wonder about you Anthony," James said with a cocked eyebrow, "you are becoming utterly Machiavellian."

"How kind of you to say so James."

"Not at all, dear fellow."

"At any rate, Hollister would hire a midwife to assist in the birth of a child, and a healthy baby named Jennifer arrives. Unfortunately, a short time after the birth, sadly, due to some unspecified complication, Sandra dies, and the death is kept secret. Not long after that, a second midwife is called to the house and being unaware of the first birth, she assists in the birth of the second child. Perhaps she is told that the sister arrived earlier, but the second child was a problem and needed help. I have no idea if this would be possible, but just let's accept that it was, and she delivers a boy whom they named Bartholomew. It is then announced with great sadness that unfortunately Sandra suffered catastrophic complications and died. And now the twins..."

"Twins?"

"Yes, they are now officially accepted as twins, and are in need of a wet-nurse. Hollister and the mistress have now cleared the way to bring another woman into the house."

"Enter the lovely Henrietta," James interjected.

"Exactly, a woman grieving after just losing her own child, and takes the position in the household as the wet-nurse. Soon after they fall in love and following an appropriate period of mourning they marry."

"So you are saying that he killed his wife."

"No, I was simply presenting a hypothesis. It is not my intention to accuse or attach blame to anyone. Giving Hollister the benefit of the doubt, he may have been quite innocent," he said, "and unable to do anything to prevent Sandra's death."

"Then again, in the solitude of his house he may have killed her," said James.

"There is that possibility, but they raised the children together for as long as they could stand it and then sent them away to school."

"Who's to say it happened any differently? Apart from you of course. That is positively diabolical."

"Isn't it? It would make for a spicy murder mystery," Anthony said, relishing the possibility.

"So, it is quite reasonable to expect that Miss Butterworth would have grown up believing Bartholomew was her twin brother."

Anthony was in his element. "I should say it is," he said with authority.

"She did mention that they were as dissimilar as coffee and tea."

"Good point. Speaking of coffee, did you take that medicine?"

"Gosh, I completely forgot about it." James wrapped his hands around the pot and smiled with relief, "It is still hot," he said, then filled their cups. Stirring the headache medicine into his and took a sip. "Dear God, that tastes awful!" He gulped it down and refreshed the cup. "The reason for the different sex and appearance was never questioned."

"Apparently it's not unusual."

"I see. However, anyone who knew Sandra before would have twigged to the truth."

"I would think so, yes."

They paused again to consider that.

After sipping from his cup Anthony said, "Perhaps their intimate circle of friends was restricted to Scotland and unaware of what happened here."

"It matters little now, I suppose. At some point, Bartholomew must have found out the truth."

"Yes, and having confessed it to his friends, it would suggest that it was something that bothered him deeply."

James finished his second cup and said, "I wouldn't be a bit surprised."

"Nor would I. I suspect that either his father or his real mother revealed the truth to him at some point."

James reflected on that thought for a moment then speculated, "That sort of revelation certainly could have done the boy irreparable harm. Perhaps it was the motivating factor in his becoming the wastrel his sister described." Staring from the window, James was imagining the lovely but vacuous Henrietta Langdon. He finished the coffee and replaced the cup on the tray. "We must go up to Scotland and confront Mrs. Butterworth with your theory."

"So, barring a complete denial from the woman, it would appear that we have solved the mystery of the Butterworth headstone inscription. Bart was at once a brother, betrothed, and a bastard as well as being illegitimate. That neatly answers your initial question."

"So it does," he said, with finality. "I am satisfied to consider that little investigation closed, and I shall now endeavour to impart that message to Miss Butterworth." James left to use the telephone in the hall.

Anthony heard the one-sided conversation and was prepared for his ill-tempered return. "The clerk at the Shield and Arms Inn said she had checked out leaving no forward address."

"I am sorry, James. What do you plan to do now?"

"We have four murders to solve and the only motive that we can be certain of, is why Fry was killed. He was a loose end and possibly the only one who could have identified the killer. As our man left no fingerprints or other evidence at the scene of his crimes, I am at a loss."

"I don't think I have ever known you to be at a loss."

"Surely not."

"Oh yes, I am fairly certain it is."

"There is always a first time," he paused again to think. "Alright, I'm going to turn our findings over to Henry Dobbs and let the Yard decide how to proceed. Then for the rest of the day, I'm going down to the Thames and draw some boats."

The telephone bell rang several times before Mrs. Findley answered it. After knocking she opened the door and said, "It's for you Colonel, and he asked for Lord Horn."

"You can't be serious."

"It's what he said, sir."

"Very well." He followed her into the hall and picked up the receiver. "Hello this is James Horn, to whom am I speaking?"

"Horn, it's Kitchener," the man said, as if speaking to an old friend. "I am calling on a most urgent matter. Are you able to speak freely?"

"Uh... Yes Sir." James was stunned to be spoken to in such an intimate way by what may have been the most powerful man in the Empire. The P.M., Herbert Henry Asquith had just appointed Field Marshal Lord Kitchener to the post of Secretary of State for War.

"Good man. Now, I knew your brother Hugh quite well, he was one of the few sober, intelligent, and dare I say, rational voices in the House of Lords. When I let it be known that I was looking for someone for this special job, my predecessor, Field Marshal Roberts, mentioned you. He said you and Hugh were as similar in temperament and intellect as peas in a pod.

"That was very kind of him, Sir."

"I won't beat about the bush here James, I am counting on that to be true. As I am certain you are aware, we are on the threshold of a war. A war of such magnitude that it will involve the entire world."

"I am in complete agreement, Sir."

"Thank heavens for that. I will be throwing the full weight of my office against this threat, and I need your help in intelligence."

"Of course, I am at your service Field Marshal."

"Excellent. My office, Whitehall, Wednesday afternoon at 2:00. Can you be there?"

"Yes Sir."

"Good, in the meantime I have arranged for you to have a chat with an old sea captain who will bring you up to date."

*****

Chapter ~ 7

Horatio Herbert Kitchener
Field Marshal Lord Kitchener

Whitehall

The meeting at the War Office was in progress when James arrived. The corporal of the guard opened the door for him and showed him to his seat at the side of the room. Having spent the previous three days in the office of the 'Captain,' James felt prepared to face almost anything. The 'Captain' was Sir Mansfield George Smith-Cumming, the man destined to lead the Directorate of Military Intelligence which would, in time, become MI5 And MI6.

James listened intently as Field Marshal Kitchener was addressing the general staff. "Gentlemen, the Germans have mobilized their army on the eastern border of the Austro-Hungarian Empire, our presumption is that this is a move to sustain the Empire for its plans in the Balkans. To provide us with some background intelligence, I have asked Lieutenant Colonel Lord James Horn, III Earl of Reedmont, to join us. He will be heading up a new bureau of MI1, under the command of Smith-Cumming and will be responsible for espionage and counter-intelligence activities at home."

James was floored by this pronouncement; he had no idea that what Kitchener had in mind would be such a large undertaking. He gladly accepted the challenge to take on this new responsibility.

"James is the brother of a highly respected member of the House of Lords, the late Hugh Richard Horn, II Earl of Reedmont. Lord James Wilson Horn was one of the senior officers in the intelligence service of the Commander in Chief India, and Commander in Chief South Africa under Lord Roberts and comes highly recommended by him. Lord James, if you will?"

"Thank you, Sir. Germany would only make such a move if the Kaiser had made some sort of assurance to support the Austro-Hungarian Empire against Serbia. We now believe that he has. It appears that they are proceeding with the Schlieffen Plan, gentlemen. If I may, Sir?"

"Carry on General."

Surprised by the instant promotion James thanked him and moved over to a space at the table with a large map of the world with the surrounding oceans painted on the surface. There was a box at the side of the table containing sets of figures and ships. White represented France, black was Germany, red was Russia's army, and blue represented the British Empire. Using the shuffleboard stick to place a few of the black figures on the eastern border of Austria- Hungary he indicated the movement of German troops.

"To simultaneously declare war on two fronts against Russia and France would be a recipe for disaster. To fool us into believing that they intend to move against Russia first that will deploy a relatively small defensive force to this position, along the Russian border. Their plan is to make a show of it while they wait for the Russians to mobilize their armies. According to Schlieffen, that should take six weeks or more and we have no reason to doubt that. It is a huge country, and we are well aware that they are not prepared for what is to come. The Russians will have to assemble, arm, and train their forces before they can commit them to battle."

Then reaching across the table, he circled neutral Belgium with his pointer, then moved a larger number of black figures to that country's border with Germany.

"Now, according to our informants in Germany, while our attentions are distracted to the east, the commander of the German Second Army, General Karl von Bülow, will lead an aggressive action against France by going through Belgium."

As he shuffled the figures into France one of the generals was shocked. "But that means that we..."

"We will be at war, yes Sir, it does," James said flatly. "Because of promises made, we will be forced at that point to declare war on Germany." His heart was pounding as the tension of the pending situation deepened.

The same general officer said, "Apparently, Roberts was correct."

"Most prophetically, yes Sir."

Another general officer asked, "Do we have any idea how long before they begin to move?"

Kitchener took that one. "There is no predictable timetable, gentlemen. But having said that, I believe that we will be at war in a fortnight at the outside."

"Great Scott man," Another general commented loudly. "You can't be serious!"

"I am deadly serious. Gentleman, we are all serious men, warriors tested in battle. It is our time to lead now, we can no longer be distracted by the incessant chatter of politicians denying the facts.

"England has become complacent, thinking that she has no stake in these territorial squabbles. Well gentlemen, Germany is determined to see to it that we do. Do not doubt that the British Empire is facing the most dangerous threat it has ever had to face. Failure in this trial will mean the end of us."

"But how sure are you that this threat is coming so soon?"

"We have had a report that Nikola Pašić, the Serbian prime minister, heard of a plot conceived by Colonel Dragutin Dimitrijević, the head of Serbia's military intelligence, to assassinate Archduke Franz Ferdinand. He tried to warn the Austrian government of it, but his message was ignored. You can be certain that whatever the result of that plot may be, there will be drastic consequences.

"The government of Austria-Hungary has been waiting for any excuse to eliminate Serbia's bid for independence. If that should happen then Serbia will have to declare war on the Empire.

"That will be the signal for Germany to put its plan into action. The moment Belgium is taken, we will be at war, and may God protect us. God save the King."

*****

The Assignment

Later in his private office, Lord Kitchener spoke with James about his plans for the new department of the SSB.

"This is where I need you James. I am counting on you to create a new force with the mission of gathering information from wherever you can find it.

"We need to know what Germany is going to bring against us. We haven't been able to set up a base of operation inside their country as yet. The SSB is dedicated to accomplishing that of course. I have heard rumours of a network of agents working for Germany's navy here in England."

"The German navy is running spy operations for them now?"

"Yes. I have been told that the Sektion III b has become a laughing stock within the Prussia's General Staff. The navy is going on its own."

"That would weaken their intelligence gathering enormously wouldn't it?"

"Not necessarily. I understand that Reinhard Scheer is to be given command of the Second Battle Squadron. Under his leadership, it is anyone's guess how long their shortfall will last. He will be desperate for a source of serviceable intelligence about our naval strategy.

"What I want you to do is set up a training facility for us and then get your agents out as quickly as possible. I have acquired a suitable location for you to assemble professional agents and begin training a new force. James, we need well trained people, men and women to work in the field abroad, and here at home. Do you think you can manage that?"

"Yes, Lord Kitchener, it will be my honour, Sir."

"Fine. With the rank of general you should be able to begin straight away."

"Of course, but Sir, if I may. If I am a general, I will not be able to perform the tasks that I need to do in order to fulfil your requirements."

"Then what do you suggest?"

"I would be better able to serve you as a field officer."

"A brigadier?"

"Yes Sir."

"Very well, Brigadier Horn, you have your orders. Let's get cracking, shall we? I shall be in touch again very soon."

****

MI-2$_H$

His first order of business was to brief Anthony on what had transpired and to promote him to Lieutenant Colonel. This new commission made him a Commanding Officer of a new branch of the SSB, called Military Intelligence, Bureau C.

Together they began calling in members of their old intelligence unit from the South African War. Some were detailed to work as instructors, some became recruiters and were sent out to universities looking for volunteers for an unspecified military detachment.

Candidates were sought out from the campuses of Oxford, Cambridge, Durham University, the University of St Andrews, University of Glasgow, Royal Holloway, and the University of Edinburgh. And the numbers of eligible candidates grew quickly. Both men and a few women volunteered and passed a thorough vetting procedure before they were told what they were in for.

Surprisingly, not one of them backed out. Most of the other volunteers were veterans of the Boer War. Those with experience in counterintelligence work were sent directly out into the field across the British Isles, to blend into their surroundings and hunt for spies.

Shortly after that, James received a second call from Lord Kitchener.

Kitchener had arranged for that facility to house his special intelligence unit, MI-2$_H$, outside of London. For the duration of the war Horn's secret intelligence school took over the Rothling Estate by Hatchard Green, temporarily displacing Lord Rothling, who moved his family to their house in London.

With their base of operations funded and supplied, Anthony and James opened the classroom doors to volunteers, code named Green Fields. Ever mindful of the unsolved Club 17 murders James made a point of keeping track of where the people involved were and what they were doing. There were two on that list that he had not as yet met. Jennifer's stepmother, Mrs. Henrietta Butterworth, who was living in a grand house just outside of Glasgow. The other was Miss Cynthia Shaw, who was also living in the Glasgow area.

He left standing orders that if any of the names on his list came up in a report, he was to be notified immediately.

MI-2$_H$ began its operations against the Central Powers.

*****

CHAPTER ~ 8

THE BLACK HAND

They strolled into the tiny bistro dressed in the street clothes of the working-class district of Belgrade, in twos and threes. Though they looked just like the men who laboured for wages, these were men of vision, of passion, lusting for power, they were dangerous men known as the Unification or Death Society.

Above: Early members of the Black Hand, (back row right)
Dragutin Dimitrijević aka Apis
Right: Signatures of Black Hand members, from the constitution dated
September 6, 1911 with official logo of the Black Hand.

They were officers in the Army of the Kingdom of Serbia who came together to unite the territories of a South Slavic majority, ruled neither by Serbia nor Montenegro. Their inspiration for this society came from the unification of Italy in 1859-1870, and also from the unification of Germany in 1871. In 1903, Apis and his fellow officers had staged a military coup in the Kingdom of Serbia to overthrow the regime. They stormed the Royal Palace in Belgrade, where they assassinated King Alexander I of Serbia and Queen Draga. Her brothers and the Prime Minister were also killed, thus wiping out the Obrenović dynasty. The coup was successful, and it ushered in the Karađorđević dynasty with Peter I taking the throne.

Their leader, Dragutin Dimitrijević, was the chief of the military intelligence section of the general staff, his fellow conspirators affectionately referred to him by his nickname Apis. He controlled their security, and his authority was unquestioned. With conceit of victory to fuel their fervour, and the hot blood of fomenting political change coursing through their veins, they turned their attention to driving the Austro-Hungarian Empire out.

After the Empire's annexation of Bosnia and Herzegovina in 1908, Dragutin Dimitrijević and the others signed their names to a constitution of their secret society, the Black Hand.

They would ultimately light the fuse that would explode into the First Great War.

The tables out front were occupied by Apis's soldiers disguised in street clothes, others were scattered about the street, keeping watch. The neighbourhood knew something was taking place in the Tuzijuić Café and didn't need to be told to keep away. As Apis stepped across the threshold, the owner, an old man named Tuzijuić, smiled slyly as he prepared espresso for a customer. André, his sous chef, pretended not to notice the leader of the society walking by.

Mushka, the attractive waitress, blew Apis a kiss from behind the bar. He acknowledged the men with a princely nod, but Mushka, he paused to stroke her cheek before passing through the curtain to the meeting room at the back.

Everyone stood in silence until he took his seat at the head of a long trestle table. "This is an auspicious moment my friends," he said. "The hour of our unification is at hand." Excited chatter filled the room. He held up his hand to calm them before he continued. "Archduke Franz Ferdinand will be going to Sarajevo to inspect their army of occupation at the end of June. I propose that we welcome him with a bomb and when he is dead, then we drive the Austro-Hungarian bastards out of Serbia forever."

To that they all stood, and raising their wine glasses they chorused their motto, "Unification or Death."

*****

CHAPTER ~ 9

THE SECRET INTELLIGENCE SERVICE

As James and Anthony were fully involved with their new duties, Consort. The Club 17 murders were left in the hands of Scotland Yard, and it seemed as though that situation was settled.

The Secret Service Bureau was renamed the Secret Intelligence Service, SIS, known generally as Military Intelligence 1, or MI-1$_C$. Cumming used his initial C, written in green ink, when signing documents and messages to maintain his anonymity and security. It quickly became the tradition in the service and James followed suit with a green H as his signature. While MI-1$_C$ began focusing its energies on the German Navy, MI-2$_H$ was doing similar work in England and training agents for the rest of Europe as well.

A great deal of information had been collected on the military build-up in Germany from members of the government, the army's general staff, and individuals who toured the country during the years and months leading up to the war.

With that intelligence in the bank, the SIS began to build the manpower it needed to meet the challenges it would face in their conflict with the Central Powers.

Germany had been building up its war machine for years, the SIS was certain that the German intelligence service, Abteilung III b had agents everywhere. But in fact, they hadn't. Unlike the SIS, Abteilung's sole concern was counterintelligence within Germany, and its limited foreign intelligence capabilities were focused on France and Russia.

The German navy, on the other hand, seemed to have a clearer eye on the threat posed by England. They knew they could not compete with the Royal Navy's Grand Fleet, and it was in England that they focused their campaign of disinformation, espionage and sabotage.

For most Brits though, those predictions Lord Roberts made of a great European war were forgotten. It was summer and as usual there were so many other entertaining things that occupied the minds of Englishmen. European troubles held little interest for them. More important they felt was the Home Rule for Ireland Conference at Buckingham Palace on the 1st of July.

Also, there was continued entertainment from the suffragette movement, which years before had declared a war of disobedience on the government. Some of their groups resorted to violent attacks which had become the staple of British newspapers.

On the 10th of July, suffragette Rhoda Fleming hopped up on the running board of the King and Queen's vehicle limousine in Perth, Scotland, much to the amusement of the papers.

But their revolution for women's rights was not about the destruction of society, it was about giving women the vote.

Great Britain seemed to be shielded from the inevitable conflict, but across the Channel the fuse was about to be lit. The leaders of the Black Hand were aware that their actions would probably lead to war between the Empire and Serbia, but they weren't able to anticipate the chain of events that would follow.

Archduke Ferdinand and his wife Sophie had travelled to Bosnia's capital, Sarajevo, to inspect his Imperial troops. Agents of the Black Hand rolled a bomb under their vehicle and though people were injured by the explosion the assassination attempt failed. The following day, at 11:15 am on June 28, the Archduke and his consort decided to make an impromptu visit to the hospital to pay their respects to a soldier who had been injured by the bomb. This time, the plot succeeded. 19-year-old Gavrilo Princip stepped up to the car and shot the royal couple dead.

Just as Lord Kitchener had predicted, the major cataclysmic event that would set it all in motion had happened. But it was not what Apis had expected at all.

Rather than pack up and leave as the Black Hand had hoped, the leaders of the Austro-Hungarian government couldn't have been more pleased. They saw this rash act as the perfect opportunity to humiliate Serbia and enhance Austria-Hungary's prestige in the Balkans. Now they could deal with the insurgents once and for all. Their plan to smack down Serbia had been on the table for some time.

James was also correct in foreseeing Kaiser Wilhelm's assurance of Germany's support. Following the assassinations, that support was confirmed by the Kaiser before he went on his annual cruise to Norway.

That gave the Austro-Hungarian government the excuse it needed to settle the question of Serbian nationalism once and for all. They presented an ultimatum to Serbia. Although its terms were unacceptable, Serbia finally capitulated on July 19.

The French Prime Minister's visit to Russia delayed the Russian response and it wasn't until after the July 24 announcement of Serbia's capitulation that the Russians raised their objections.

Then the next day Serbia replied to the ultimatum, accepting most of its demands but protesting against two of them—namely, that Serbian officials (unnamed, but widely accepted that they referred to Apis, and the secret society Union or Death) should be dismissed at Austria-Hungary's behest and that Austro-Hungarian officials should take part, on Serbian soil, in proceedings against organizations hostile to Austria-Hungary. Serbia wanted to take it to international arbitration, but Austria-Hungary severed diplomatic relations and ordered a partial mobilization.

India was beginning to strengthen its push to drive the British out. The British Empire's forces were already stretched to the limits in Africa and James was not alone as he wondered if they had the resources to sustain them as they were pulled into another war.

Finally, reality dawned on the people of Great Britain.

As predicted, following the Schlieffen Plan, Germany attacked neutral Belgium, and Britain had no choice but to declare war on Germany.

****

More Club 17 Victims

As young men swarmed the streets of London celebrating the outbreak of war, the eight surviving members of the Enlightened Twelve were quick to return to their regiment. While preparing for war, the army was acquiring more vehicles to carry the fight to the enemy and training the new recruits in their use.

Coming off the farms and from small villages to London and driving any vehicle was a completely new experience.

Large transport lorries and ambulances were especially difficult, so it was not surprising that there would be accidents and fatalities.

On the 16th, two such accidents took place within hours of each other claiming the lives of two young lieutenants. Though in completely different locations they had both been crossing a street when they were hit and killed. One was run over by a troop transport lorry while the other fell victim of a military bus.

James had missed the report in the papers and was alerted to their deaths by a military notice warning its members to be extra cautious when working near motor vehicles. He called a friend in the Royal Military Police, Major Richard Priest, to ask for the identities of the men.

"Well for goodness sakes if it isn't the old African Ghost. James, how are you?

"Well but overworked once again. Richard, I just saw that two officers were killed in separate incidents."

"You are referring to the recent bus and lorry accidents."

"Exactly. Could you confirm the names for me, please?"

"Of course, lieutenants Adam Huxley and Brian Conroy. Do the names mean anything to you?"

"Unfortunately, they do, yes." He paused for a moment to formulate his next question. "Richard, did they have anything on their persons after the accidents, such as a note perhaps, or a scrap of paper which contained a symbol?"

"How odd that you should know about that. Yes, each man had a calling card with nothing but two arrows printed on it, one pointing down and the other to the left. It seemed strangely familiar, but we couldn't for the life of us understand what it meant. Is it some sort of club?"

"In a manner of speaking. For want of a better name, I call the symbol the Traitor's Brand.

"That sounds ominous. Oh, dash-it-all, that's it. A brand, yes, I recall it now, a horse released by us then claimed by the Boer."

"Right, and ominous it is. It has been found on all the victims so far."

"So far...? You mean you expect more to come?"

"I do, six more to be exact. It was a case Hillman and I had been working before this mess started. I suspect that the cards were placed on the bodies after they were killed. My guess is that neither was accidental, and the drivers were not who they said they were. It also confirms that my suspicions were right. What we are dealing with here, Richard, is a team of professional killers."

"But what possible reason would they have for murdering these men?"

"My senses tell me that they must have witnessed something that the killer did or said. I have questioned them all, and apparently they are unaware of it. All we have at the moment is that, as you guessed, all the victims were members of a club and a group. The club was Club 17, and the group was called the Enlightened Twelve."

"That seems rather pretentious."

"To know them is to understand the definition of pretension. All were together in South Africa and captured at the same time by the Boer. Only eleven of them eventually came home, and now there are just six left."

"Good heavens, but this is a matter for the civil police."

"The Yard is dealing with it, and I would be grateful if you would pass this information along to them. I had been working closely with Superintendent Dobbs."

"I will inform him of course."

"I appreciate that, Richard."

"James, I hesitate to ask, but I heard that you are Lord Horn now. Are you playing on the same team again, or are you moving into the House?"

"Still with intelligence, the SIS but that's all I can say."

"Well then say no more. We'll talk again, no doubt."

"No doubt."

*****

CHAPTER ~ 10

THE LADY SUISSE

An analyst monitoring Lord Horn's residence in London sent an urgent report to the Commander of MI-C, informing him that a telephone call had been received there which originated in Geneva, Switzerland. It was thought that it might be from one of the SIS agents reporting on the situation in Germany, but Lt. Col. Anthony Hillman knew it must have come from Miss Jennifer Butterworth.

Miss Jennifer Butterworth.

Passing the information up through channels, it arrived on Brigadier Horn's desk. So much has happened since he had sent her to that Inn at King's Cross that it seemed as though it was from another life.

"Miss Butterworth, I am surprised to hear from you again. May I ask why you disappeared so suddenly?"

"Col. Horn, I am sorry that I didn't respond to your messages.

The reason was that someone had tracked me down to that inn. I don't know how, perhaps I was followed, but it doesn't matter now."

"Oh, why is that?" James asked.

"My driver was able to... Well to put him off, he said. I'm not sure what that meant, and he wouldn't give me any details. He insisted that we leave England immediately and not to trust anyone."

"You spoke to this man in person? Did he identify himself to you?"

"He never got close to me, thank goodness. I was so frightened that Kirk stepped in and took care of that on his own. He said the man identified himself as a government agent. Kirk thought the man was Swiss because he spoke Swiss German, but then when the man drew a pistol..."

"Are you safe in Geneva?" James asked.

"Why wouldn't I be? It is a neutral country."

"So was Belgium, and we now know what Germany thinks of their neutrality. Kirk was right to get you away, but I don't think Switzerland was the right choice."

"If not here, then where?"

"I doubt that Germany's army will ever cross the channel. You should be here. I have an old family estate outside of London where you could stay."

"Thank you for thinking of my security, and for your advice, but if the danger is linked to my association with you then perhaps I must make other arrangements on my own."

"Does that mean ...? Wait, don't tell me. Perhaps you are right after all, and you should avoid any further contact with me."

"Thank you for all you have done for me, Colonel," Jennifer said, "you have been most kind."

James replaced the handset to its hanger and sat back.

"What do you think she will do now?" Anthony asked.

"I have no earthly idea, but I don't have the time to worry about that. She must make her own choices now."

"She did provide us with serviceable intelligence though."

"Yes, she did. There is no doubt now that a cell of German operatives is acting on Britain's soil. They are the ones who are bent on eradicating the Enlightened Twelve, and I wish to Hell I knew why!"

*****

132

PART~2

SPIES AND SABOTEURS

CHAPTER ~ 11

1901 IN AMSTERDAM

Long before the war in South African was over, the British Empire's enemies were planning for a war to end all wars. Their plans were so well laid out, so well-rehearsed, that victory was practically a certainty.

Lars Himmershold was a rather rakish figure of a man in his forties. A scholar, he was intelligent and charming, and though his parents were working class he had the bearing of nobility. Lars had an uncanny gift with people, he understood how people thought, and how to motivate them, and the wit to use his gift to manipulate them. There

Lars Himmershold

was an air of authority about him that commanded attention and people were eager to listen to him. These were the attributes that brought him to the attention of the ruling class. He moved in that rarefied circle occupied by the most powerful people in Germany.

Among them was Alfred Graf von Schlieffen, the chief of the German general staff who readily saw his potential.

Germany's intelligence agency Sektion III b was inefficient and needed rejuvenation. Schlieffen understood that to succeed with his plan for European domination he needed a better system of intelligence gathering, and at one of the government gatherings he asked Himmershold how he would do it. Himmershold said they should try to recruit some of the people from the ranks of their enemies.

Count Schlieffen found his answer fascinating, and as the conversation continued the idea of building such a group soon became a reality, an experiment in the art of convincing a man to turn against everything he stood for and pledge his allegiance to his enemy.

There was already an ample supply of British soldiers in Boer prisoner camps, and they were the perfect subjects for his experiments. The Chief of the Imperial German General Staff gave Himmershold the chance to develop a test program and the academic chose Cape Town as his laboratory.

The war was going poorly for the Boers, but for this experiment, there was a treasure trove of captured British officers. They were routinely interrogated by the Boer generals, often using cruel and painful methods, but information was difficult to elicit. Himmershold used a different approach. He brought his special blend of inducement to the problem. For a select group of wounded men, he offered promises of medical treatment, and very significant rewards for cooperation. There was no suggestion of torture or further deprivation. If they refused to cooperate they were shot.

What better way to turn a man, heart, mind, and soul than to offer him, not only care, food, and water, but life beyond simply survival. Life on a level they had never dreamed of.

He offered this approach to the select few that he had studied and found susceptible to his influence.

He appealed to their dissatisfaction with Mother England and encouraged the feeling that their country had somehow let them down and abandoned them.

They had been sent to Africa to lay down their lives simply to make the greedy upper class Englishmen wealthier. His approach was very convincing to the right men because there was a great deal of truth to be found in his propaganda. A few of his test subjects proved to be of stronger character than he anticipated.

Himmershold admired loyalty, he also appreciated an inherent problem in allowing loyal Brits to talk about what had gone on in his clinic, so their reward for this loyalty to King and Country was a bullet in the head. Those few men who did accept his vision of the world would prove to be far more useful to Germany than to the Afrikaans' failing struggle. The few men he turned could be invaluable should a war with England come about.

There was one young officer who was very keen to switch sides, just the sort of man who could be persuaded to do just about anything for the right reward. Himmershold promised him a new name, a home in Amsterdam, wealth, and special training for his personal brand of warfare. His new name was Dagg Hartogg.

There was a second man that was captured at the same time, though his wound was much more serious. The two men were friends, and Himmershold saw that offering to save the life of this second man would sweeten the prize. It did, and he was given the name Arnold Bleck. They were moved from the field hospital to his modern, clean facility near Cape Town. When they were stable and could safely be moved a long distance they were taken to Amsterdam for medical attention.

Bleck survived but he was nothing more than a shell of a man who could walk, eat and drink and that was about all. He was there because his childhood friend insisted that he be kept alive and Dagg Hartogg saw to it that he was cared for.

Though von Schlieffen retired and was replaced in 1906, Himmershold's program continued, keeping to the same course laid out for European domination.

The house on Bloedstraat, third door on the right.

Over the next few years Hartogg and Bleck shared an apartment in Amsterdam's Red District on Bloedstraat. As a cover for his activities, Hartogg was caring for his friend while working for Lars von Himmershold as a junior partner in his import-export business. That allowed him to travel all over western Europe and eventually across to England. At that time, he was able to explain his prolonged absence and re-establish himself in London as a loyal Englishman with business interests in Europe.

*****

A Threat In Glasgow

It was late in the evening of Friday, August 14, 1914, when the message came in from the west coast of Scotland. The third phase of the Battle of the Frontiers was under way and the French had moved against German forces near Sarrebourg, at the beginning of the Battle of Lorraine. And the war had spread all the way across continent to Asia.

The attention of MI-1C and MI-2H was spread so thinly that important information was being dropped. MI-1 heard that light cruiser SMS Emden had left the Imperial German Navy in the Pacific and set course for the major shipping lanes between Singapore, Colombo and Aden. Rebel forces were trying to capture Albania's capital Durrës, but Romanian volunteers were forcing them back. Another report came from much closer to home, from Scotland.

The report was filed from the Glasgow office about suspicious activity on the river Clyde. It reported that a small fishing vessel was found beached at Cardwell Bay near Gourock.

Josh Fellows, the agent in charge in Glasgow, instructed that it was to be delivered immediately. But it didn't reach James' desk until noon the following day.

When James opened it, he was furious. The delay could have meant a lost opportunity. The locals knew every ship and dory that plied their waters, and this one was not one of theirs. Fellows had given it a thorough examination and found the builder's mark, it was German, built in Wilhelmshaven, close to Hamburg on the shore of Jade Bight. He was certain that the German agent would have gone from there up to Glasgow. It was one tiny piece of information, but his report contained a detail that hit James like a hammer. A local fisherman by the name Brian Bean mentioned two names that James had not heard in some time.

"I was on the dock mending my nets," Innis said, "when this Englishman approached me, and as bold as you please, he asked me if I'd run him up to Glasgow! 'What?' says I, and he repeats the question. So, I says, 'I doanno.' Then, I decided to give it a bit of a thought, then asked him when he wanted to go. 'Right now,' says he. 'Are you mad?' says I. He was speaking to me like I was running some 'effing taxi service. The bleedin' nerve of the man. He was English, so I suppose there was no great surprise to me, his being a daft..." He caught a stiff look from the agent.

"Oh, pardon me for that one. I tells the man. 'It'll be getting dark within the hour,' I tells him. 'It's important that I get there tonight, says he.' So, I hems and haws until he says, 'Name your price." Quick as fox I says, 'Five pounds before you set a foot on my deck,' I tells him, 'that's my price.' And what do you think he done? 'Done,' says he, and hands me five pounds before I could wink."

Calmly the agent asked, "So you did?"

"Did I?" The fisherman asked.

"I am asking you; did you take him to Glasgow? A simple yes or no will suffice."

"Well as a matter of fact I did. I sailed him up the Clyde and put him to shore on the beach at the mouth of the river Kelvin. Then off he goes, into the dark without so much as a thanks. Bloody English."

"By any chance, did he give you his name?" Fellows asked.

"He didn't offer it, but I did hear him use his name when he thought I weren't listening. I thought nothing of it at the time, but now that you are asking questions about him, I guess I should have reported it. You see, he went below and set up a little radio transmitter. I heard every word he said, as clear as I am hearing you now. It's like that on the river, you can hear the voices from shore like they was right here on the deck.

"'Shaw,' he said, 'it's Hartogg,' and then he said, 'I am in Scotland now and I'm on my way to you. I will make contact tomorrow.' Then he said something queer. He said, 'Stay in place.' Now what do you suppose he meant by that? Whoever was on the other end of that wire said nary a word. The man switched off the radio and packed it away in his kit."

"Are you certain that those are the only names you heard?"

"Aye, Shaw and Hartogg."

"Did he say anything about where he would contact Shaw?"

"No, 'twas just as I told you, nothing more."

"Hartogg is a Dutch name, yet you said he was English."

"I knows an Englishman when I hears him lad."

Seeing those names in the report brought it all back to James, the young man Arthur Shaw was supposed to have died in a Boer prison camp. But who the hell was Hartogg?

It is odd how some small act or happenstance can change the course of one's life. Before being confronted with murder, James only thought was how curious that silly inscription was. Brother, Betrothed, Bastard. Now it was clear that all along he had been dealing with a murderous cell of traitors and spies working for Germany.

*****

Butterworth Mansion, Glasgow

There were 4.8 million Scots at last count and who is to say how many of them felt that, if it weren't for the threat from Germany, they, like the Irish, would rather be an independent country.

James and Anthony took the train to Glasgow, appearing as ordinary as any two businessmen on a sales call. They chose a small inn and kept a low profile as they waited to meet with Josh Fellows. The meeting was very brief as the only thing he had to report was that Mr. Bean had taken the time to sit down with a sketch artist who came up with a drawing of Mr. Hartogg. It was printed and handed around, but there had been no sightings of the man.

There was little point to hiding who they were, people were gossiping about the two boys up from London for a look see. James was somewhat amused to be referred to as a boy, but it was frustrating. He thought they couldn't go anywhere without people shielding their chattering mouths behind their hands as they talked about them. It was like a fox on the hunt through the forest with the jays following in the treetops calling out their warning.

Anthony arranged for a staff car to pick them up for a drive in the countryside. If they weren't getting leads in the city they may as well go out and interview the twin's stepmother. Their driver knew the area very well and headed south to Butterworth House, a mansion in Dumbreck.

A short trip through the rough tenements took them to a country field, marking the end of the city, and from then on, the driver followed a private lane through a forested part of the estate. Their first view of Butterworth House was at the end of Lime Avenue, a long tree-lined cart path, and it was indeed a grand country house, perched on the banks of a small river called White Cart Water.

"Have we come to the right address?" Anthony asked the driver.

"Aye Sir, 'tis Butterworth House and that's a fact. I'd often come here with me Da when I were a wee lad. He worked in the gardens for old man Butterworth."

"Then I propose that we dismount and make the rest of our way on foot. Stay with the car Sergeant."

"Aye Sir."

"If she grew up here it is hard to believe that she would avoid returning to this place."

"What I find hard to believe, is that she let her stepmother keep it," said Anthony.

As they walked down the short slope to the courtyard a maid opened the door and stared out at them as if they were from another planet. She looked nervous, an indication that all was not right within.

A moment later she was pulled away and replaced by the butler, who stood as if his presence alone provided more security than a platoon of soldiers. Anticipating a less than warm welcome, James stopped. A pace or two later, Anthony came to a halt.

"Are ya lost, gentleman?" he asked sternly.

The Butterworth butler, Mr. Perch

"So much for the legendary Scottish warmth and hospitality," Anthony whispered.

"Hush," James whispered back. "I shouldn't like to be turned away after coming this far." Clearing his throat, he responded as pleasantly as possible, "Not if this is Butterworth House."

"Who be ya and what d'ya want?" asked the butler, with an accent and vocabulary that as far as Anthony was concerned, should have required a translator.

"What did he say?"

"Oh, my God, if you of all people can't understand him why the devil would you expect me to?"

"A good point. If he was my butler I'd kick him down the steps."

"Oh, do shut up, Anthony, you are not helping."

"Whit's thon ya say? Ah dinnae hear ya."

"I said, I am Brigadier Horn…"

Frowning, Anthony whispered, "Oh, so you can understand him."

James glared at him again, "…and with me is Private Hillman."

"Hey!"

"We have come from London, on a matter of the utmost urgency, to speak with Mrs. Butterworth. Would you inform her that we are here?"

Without worrying about giving offence, the butler said, "Och, she already ken, ya daft Englishman. Aye, mon eff ya must." They just stood there wondering what he said, so he stepped aside and waved them in.

Dripping with insincerity James said, "You are too kind." To which Anthony snorted. Ignoring him, James asked, "And your name would be…?"

"Rodney Perch," the old man said, closing the door gently. "Bide, while I announce ya. And mind, the eejit dug bites."

They discovered that he was referring to the small white terrier curled up by the door. It didn't move a hair.

"Is it even alive?" Anthony asked."

"Whit's thon ya say?" Perch asked.

"I shan't move a muscle," James replied. Anthony snorted again. There was plenty of time to investigate the hall from their vantage point.

Carved crowns with bows and clusters of fruit decorated the panelled walls. An interesting chandelier made up of a cluster of illuminated sets of deer antlers lit the hall, and a huge skull and antlers of an ancient elk hung on the landing wall. Beneath them the ornately carved oak staircase rose up from the black and white marble floor."

"Very homey."

"If you like country living, I suppose," James said.

Presently they heard a lady's footsteps on the stairs and looked up, expecting an attractive elderly woman to appear. But instead, she was much younger and very familiar.

"I hadn't planned on you discovering my little secret, Mr. Horn," she said, from the landing.

"I must admit that I had not planned it either, Miss Butterworth. Why the deception?"

She bristled. "It wasn't my intention to deceive you, sir. In fact, my coming here was your idea."

"My idea? How intriguing, tell me more."

"With pleasure. I thought that perhaps your concern for my safety in Switzerland was justified, so I packed up my things came here straight away."

"Then why did you not inform me of this?"

"You told me not to tell you. I do wish you would make up your mind Colonel."

"Uh yes, I had quite forgotten that, forgive me. By the by, the rank is Brigadier now..."

"Oh, how lovely for you. How interesting though."

"What is?"

"Your promotion. I didn't know that private detectives had ranks nor that they could promote themselves."

"They don't obviously, and it would be silly if they could. I would have thought you were aware that we are at war with Germany, among others, and so Anthony and I are once again in the army."

Her smile slipped just a little. "I see. Army intelligence, wasn't it?"

He didn't answer that question. "Moving on, I am just surprised to find you here with your stepmother. I was under the impression that you were not on good terms."

"Yes, I said that I loathed her, didn't I. Well as a matter of fact, I don't anymore and, as it happens, I am here alone. Henrietta married again and lives in my house in the south of France. Butterworth House is all mine again."

"I see. You failed to mention that Mrs. Butterworth had... How shall I put it?"

"Moved on?" Her smile brightened measurable. "Yes, well I failed to mention a number of things when last we met. I can't tell you how lovely it is to be back home after so many years away. How are you Mr. Hillman?"

"Quite well, thank you, Miss Butterworth. This is rather grand."

"Isn't it." She seemed quite cheerful. "It's simply amazing what great gads of guineas will do for one, isn't it?"

"To be sure." James wondered what had changed, that she could act so frivolously now. It was as if she was a completely different woman.

"What, pray tell, brings you two gentlemen to my door today?"

"We had some questions for Henrietta Butterworth..."

"Yes, the name is familiar to me, James. For a change why not dispense with all the formality and simply use first names?"

"... but since she is in the south of France it seems that our trip has been wasted."

"Now I've hurt your feelings and you are going to run off without sitting down for a decent conversation." She pouted.

"Miss Butterworth…"

"Jennifer, please."

"Whatever game you are playing at, I need you to stop it at once. As I have already told you, our country is at war, and we have some very serious questions that require serious and truthful answers."

"But you just implied that you had no questions for me. What am I to make of that, I ask you?"

"Alright, since you want me to question you, I shall. You said you failed to tell us a number of things. What exactly did you mean by that?"

"A lady must have her secrets," she said coyly, as she continued down the stairs. "It's a little game I play, if truth be told, designed to separate friend from foe. Which are you?"

His mood was clearly growing darker. "I thought we had dispensed with the games."

"Perhaps I have, James, and now it is you who is playing about."

"Absolute rubbish."

"You haven't answered my question."

"Why don't we discover the answer to that question together?"

"Meaning?"

"Meaning, what if I arrest you and take you to our Glasgow HQ to continue the questioning there?"

"You wouldn't."

"Yes, I certainly would. Does that answer your question?"

That sobered her up and the smile vanished. "I suppose it does. What would you like to know?"

She walked to the large sitting room at the front, and they followed. She sat, so they sat as well.

"Could one of the things you chose to withhold from us in London, be that you knew all along that Bart was not your twin but your half brother?"

"Uh hah. Yes, to be fair, I suppose I should have mentioned that. It was a little bit of family history that Bart shared with me. I confronted my father, and he confirmed it."

"I noticed the painting in the adjoining room, I take it that is your mother."

"No, that was... There you see, you were about to catch me in another lie. It is. She is quite beautiful, isn't she?"

"Without doubt. Has she actually remarried and is now living in your house in Saint Tropez?"

"No. Sadly she did not, and she is upstairs in bed. She's been unwell for weeks. The doctor has no idea what is wrong with her, and to be perfectly honest, she has me quite worried."

"Why all the lies, Jennifer?"

"Practically everything I told you in London was true. I was frightened, I still am. That letter from a 'friend', it terrified me. You were right, it was a threat, and I knew..."

"That you had to comply or lose your fortune."

"How would you have known that?"

"It was a simple matter of deduction. We were going to ask Henrietta which child she birthed. Was it Bart as you claimed in London, or was it you?"

"And now you know."

"It was Anthony who came up with the idea that both Sandra and Henrietta were pregnant at the same time."

"Most kind of you to mention me, James."

"Anthony, must you play the ass all the time? That little confluence of fate afforded the opportunity for Henrietta and your father to perpetrate their crime..."

"How dare you! There was no crime! A deception yes, but it was not a crime."

"It doesn't matter now. I would say that things worked themselves out as they did for a reason. Whatever family problems you had, died with your father's first wife and your half bother Bart. The problem we are facing now, is of far greater concern."

"And that is?"

"As it was in the beginning. We must find the man who committed that first murder a-year-and-a-half ago. The reason for it was, I am now sure, to hide his identity. He was recognized and had to silence his victims."

"Victims?"

"Yes, all the men in their little group of twelve. They all knew him and for that they had to die. No longer is it just a matter of murder. As long as that man is alive, the survival of our nation is at risk. We must find him before he does what he came here to do."

"He is a spy?"

"Oh, he is more than that, he is a saboteur, and a deranged and despicable traitor. Bart knew he should have been the true heir to Butterworth Shipping and felt cheated."

"But he wasn't cheated at all. Father knew what a fool Bart was. There was never a chance that he would let him ruin the business."

"I have no doubt that that is true."

"How generous."

"When was it that he told you this? Was it just before he joined the army?"

"How could you have known that?"

"You mentioned that you had a letter from him before he embarked, and I am now very glad that we came and found you here today."

That surprised Anthony. "Are you, James? I'm afraid you've lost me there."

"Yes, it just came to me. Jennifer, you are still in need of protection, and as strange as it may sound, I believe that your brother is the one who has placed you in danger."

"That is impossible, my brother is dead."

"Yes... Well nevertheless, you are in danger. By any chance would one of your friends be Cynthia Shaw?"

"Cynthia? Yes of course, a dear friend. She was engaged to Bart for a time but broke it off when he went to South Africa."

"Are you aware if she is living or dead?"

"Good-Lord, what a question? She is very much alive. I lunched with her last week."

"Where is she now?"

"James, I haven't the faintest idea. She has a house in Glasgow by the... Oh ..." She paused for a second and her tone betrayed her concern. "Is she in danger too?"

"I can't say, we simply need to talk to her. It would be very helpful if you could tell us exactly where to find her."

"As you wish, she lives on Hamilton Drive, the house with the bright blue door. Shall I telephone her to tell her you're on your way?"

"No, absolutely not," James said swiftly, "I would rather you didn't do that. It would be best if she didn't know we were going to pay her a visit."

"I see. I thought you were only teasing me about being back with army intelligence and your promotions, but it's all true, isn't it."

"Yes, and I must warn you again that this is not a game, we are at war."

"Yes, I can see that now. So, you'll just sneak up on her as you did me." James began to protest. "No-no-no, I am sorry," she said, quickly revising her comment, "I only meant that I understand perfectly. I suppose everyone is a suspect these days. It might be easier to find her at one of her suffragette meetings at Union Hall. She has become such a firebrand for the cause. Women should have the vote, and so on. With so much else going on now, I thank God that business has calmed down."

"Is she a militant?"

"Gracious no! She is the most gentle woman I know. Please be kind to her."

"We must get back to the city," he said, without acknowledging her request. "We will return in due course, in the meantime, I am going to leave a guard posted at the gate to keep an eye on the house."

"Is it really necessary?"

"I believe it is. Please resist the urge to leave the house or to call your friend. You are in grave danger, Jennifer, remember that."

Without waiting for her response, they exited.

Just before leaving Butterworth House

James instructed the sergeant to stand guard and not to let anyone in or out of the house. Seeing the look of concern on the soldier's face, he assured him that his relief would be along soon.

Turning to Anthony, he said, "Now, please, be a good sport and tell me can you drive that damned thing back to Glasgow."

*****

CHAPTER ~ 12

EVENTS IN GLASGOW

Anthony left James at the HI-1 office and returned to London to select the agents from Rowling Green he needed at Glasgow. Arming them with the latest semi-automatic pistols and copies of the photograph of the man calling himself Dagg Hartogg. They took the train back to Scotland.

The picture was taken the year before he joined the army, so his people had to account for the substantial changes that would have taken place over the intervening

Bart in 1900

years. Hoping that he would lead them to the rest of the cell, their orders were to spot him, but not to engage.

Enough time had passed since his voyage up the Clyde for James to suspect that he may have already made contact with Cynthia. Finding her quickly was imperative, so in company with agent Josh Fellows, he found the house with the blue door.

Jennifer had insisted that Cynthia Shaw was not a violent woman; headstrong and determined to achieve voting rights for women perhaps, but her struggle was a peaceful one.

Of course, the woman would say that about her friend, but it didn't mean that it was true. It was possible that their suspect was in the house and most likely armed. He could even be holding her hostage, so their approach was cautious. Leaving the car at the corner they ambled along as if they were just out for a stroll.

When they approached the house, they scanned the windows to see if they were being watched but saw nothing.

As soon as they were by the gate they moved in quickly.

James stood to one side, behind the fixed door panel with his revolver ready.

Fellows knocked.

"Hang on," said a cheerfully sweet voice, "be there in a tick." The door opened and they were greeted by a young woman wiping her flour coated hands off on her apron. Fellows' immediate response to seeing her was, 'how could anything so lovely be a villain?'

"Oh hello," she said, as she tried and failed to rub

Cynthia Shaw

a smudge of flour off her nose "What can I do for you?" Fellows drew his gun and she backed away. "Oh God, how ridiculous," she said, as bold as brass. "Listen, if you have come to rob me, I'm afraid that you will be sadly disappointed."

James stepped into view with his revolver pointing at her. That startled her enough to make her jump back. Looking past her, he asked, "Is there anyone else in the house?"

"N-no. What is the meaning of this?"

"Just answer the question please."

"I said no, I am quite alone."

"Are you Miss Cynthia Shaw?" James moved forward, as Fellows remained where he was, vigilant and silent.

"I am, and who the hell are you lot?"

"Never mind that. Is there anyone else in the house?"

"I just told you twice, there isn't anyone else here. Now come on, who are you?"

"May we come in?"

"It doesn't look as though I have much choice, does it?"

"No, you don't." James spoke with a coldness reserved for the enemy. Whatever humour he may have had with Jennifer was no longer in evidence and his expression was grim. "Hold her, so she doesn't run off." He pushed by her as Fellows grabbed her arm.

"Ouch, you're hurting me."

He relaxed his grip slightly and forced her back into the house and James and kicked the door closed with the heel of his shoe.

James pointed to a chair in the parlour. "Sit her there."

Fellows directed her to the chair, but she wouldn't sit. James went into the kitchen and looked around for any sign that someone else had been there. A cigarette, a second cup of tea. All he saw was the bread dough she had been kneading and flour scattered about the kitchen table. Doubt was beginning to filter into his mind.

"I insist that you answer my question."

Speaking from the kitchen he answered her. "You can insist all you want, Miss Shaw, but my questions are the only ones that interest me for the moment."

Fellows cut in. "Have you been visited recently?"

"No."

"A gentleman caller perhaps?"

"I said, NO! And what the devil are you suggesting? How dare you ask me such a thing?!"

James returned to the parlour. "Stand down, Fellows. His phrasing may have left the wrong impression. I do apologize," said James. "Please, sit."

She refused.

"Very well. We have reason to believe that you have been in contact with a man suspected of espionage and murder. We also have reason to believe that you may be in league with him ..."

"What?"

"... and are in fact giving aid and comfort to the enemy in this house."

"That's absurd. Giving aid and..." She was trembling and looked faint. "What are you going on about?"

"Please, have a seat Miss Shaw." She sat. "Fellows, would you please give the house a thorough search."

"Sir." The agent hurried upstairs and began looking in closets, though drawers, under and behind everything she owned hoping to find a radio. It was a noisy endeavour, and he wasn't being careful with anything he touched. Downstairs, James quietly began his interrogation.

"Alright, two nights ago we believe that you received a radio message...?"

"I ... uh a what? I don't have a radio," she replied, showing a great deal of grit.

"You maintain that you did not receive a message?"

"I do. As I said, I have no radio."

"Humm." He studied her for a few seconds, an unnerving ordeal for the young woman. "I warn you, lying to me is a very bad idea. Did you receive a radio message from a man named Hartogg?"

"Still no radio. And I have no idea who this Hedgehog person is."

He had to admire her strength to be able to maintain her wit at a time like this. He smiled. "Actually, the name is Hartogg."

"Oh, terribly sorry, no offence intended. No, I have never heard that name before. It's Dutch, isn't it? It sounds Dutch."

There was a crash upstairs. She looked up at the ceiling "What in heaven's name is that man doing?"

"He is looking for your radio."

"Well, if he finds one I will be very surprised indeed. I keep telling you, I don't have a radio, and if I did, I certainly wouldn't keep it under the wash basin. You will replace, that won't you?"

"When was the last time you heard from your brother?"

"Oh, dear Lord. If you know anything about him at all, then you must know that he died in South Africa."

James looked over his shoulder as Fellows returned shaking his head. James nodded. "What if I told you that I have good reason to believe that he did not die there."

"Oh, this must be some cruel joke. It is, isn't it?"

"I assure you; I am being perfectly serious."

She looked at him expectantly. "Are you telling me that he is alive? Is that what you are saying? Oh, oh dear, but that's wonderful. Where is he? Have you had him hidden away somewhere all this time? Why did you leave me to think that he was dead?" She began to cry. "This is absolutely horrid; how dare you tell me this way. I want to see him. I must see him right away! I want to see Arthur now. Take me to him."

"Miss Shaw, control yourself. We do not have your brother."

"I don't understand. If he was alive then he would have come to me first. He is my brother, he is..."

"Miss Shaw."

She stopped and looked from James to Fellows and back again. "Oh, I see. Then he isn't alive, you just made that up to see how I would react."

"We believe that he walked into a building under his own power. With him was a man he trusted, a man with whom he had been imprisoned, and then set free. That man in whom Arthur had placed his trust, suddenly and violently betrayed him. Moments after he entered that building, Dagg Hartogg murdered him in cold blood."

"No!"

"Yes. Arthur Shaw was murdered by his friend in order to erase the killer's identity forever. His death was made to look like the killer's suicide."

"Oh God, please stop this."

"And it almost worked."

"Why are you doing this? Don't you think I have suffered enough?"

"I am telling you this, so that you understand that the man I believe you are protecting, is a vile and vicious killer, a traitor to his country. And I warn you, that if you continue protecting him you will found as guilty as he and face a firing squad alongside him."

"I am protecting no one." James didn't say anything, he just stared at her, weakening her confidence. "I am telling you the truth!"

"Are you?" He paused. "How do you expect me to believe you when we have a witness who heard him speak to you over the radio, he mentioned you by name."

"It didn't happen, your witness is wrong. I don't know anything about this man Hartogg. And as your man here will tell you, I don't have a radio." Seeing no less intensity in his eyes, her will weakened further. "You must believe me, you simply must."

"Listen to me, if you are going to have any chance of surviving this, you will cooperate, help me find this man!"

"Cooperate? I have done nothing but cooperate. If I could help you arrest the man who murdered Arthur, don't you think I would? But I don't know this Hartogg person. I have no idea who he is."

"I think you do. I think you are doing a good job of play acting but I believe that you have been a part of his plan for some time now."

"Do you? Do you?! Well then, tell me this, why on God's green earth would I help the man who murdered my brother!"

"Because he is your fiancé." She gasped. "Bartholomew Butterworth!" He was relentless.

It seemed like she might faint. "This can't be true," she said, steadying herself. She looked at James as new tears welled up in her eyes. "Oh God." She spoke as she remembered the man she had once loved. "Yes, Bart was a selfish, silly arrogant man and yes mean spirited as well, but would he kill Arthur? I can't believe it."

"Is that what he told you?"

"He hasn't told me anything. How could he, he's dead too."

"No, he is very much alive and here in Glasgow."

"No!" Her voice softened, "No. Why would he come here? Before Bart went off to that ridiculous war, I told him that I never wanted to see him again." She began looking about her as if seeking some way of escape.

"No, this can't be real, it has to be some awful dream. None of this is really happening. It can't be."

"Did he tell you why he did it, and did you then forgive him?"

"You must stop this now. Please, I can't take anymore."

"Do you honestly want me to believe that you knew nothing of this?"

Her rage swelled up again. "Of what?" she screamed. "Of what? This lie that you are telling? You are trying to get me to confess to a nightmare." She swallowed back her tears. Then all of a sudden she stopped, and her anger and frustration turned to a renewed sense of loss. "Oh God, did Bart really kill my brother?" She met his eyes unflinchingly. "He did, didn't he? So, Arthur is... He's really gone." Her body seemed to sink into itself. "It feels like he has been taken from me for the second time."

"Butterworth succeeded for a long while to make people believe he had shot himself. But it is Arthur that lies in his grave. Your brother was a sacrificial lamb, shot through the head."

"Stop it."

"His face was destroyed, so that he was unrecognisable."

"I said, stop it!"

"So that people would assume that he was Bartholomew Bigelow Butterworth slumped there, in that chair."

"You are a monster. I'm pleading with you, stop it now. Please, just stop talking."

"That I will not do, because you were a willing party to this crime."

"I wasn't." Breathing was becoming more difficult for her. "Why are you doing this? Why are you being so cruel to me?"

"Cynthia Shaw, you are under arrest for..."

"My God, you can't do this to me! I can't bear anymore."

"... accessory to murder, espionage and other crimes against..."

"No! Please just leave me alone. Please," she said, then completely broke down and sobbed.

In that instant, James' sense of compassion re-awakened and he realised just how utterly heartless and nasty he had been to her. He had been pressing so hard because he really had no evidence to support any of his charges, he simply expected her to break down, and confess all. But this could not be an act. He had to acknowledge now that she had been telling the truth.

"Alright."

"What's this now? Are you saying that you believe me?"

"Yes, I believe you. I am sorry for how hard I pushed you, but I had to be sure. You are innocent and this interrogation is over. Fellows, do you think you could make Miss Shaw a cup of tea?"

"Yes Sir."

"I don't want any tea, thank you. What I want is for you both to leave now."

"We will, very soon, but there are one or two things left to take care of."

"What could possibly be left that you haven't already destroyed?"

"Have you a picture of Bart?"

She looked up at him, her once lovely face was now red and swollen from crying, but her eyes were still filled with rage. "What?"

"A picture of your fiancé, do you have one?"

"Of course, I do."

"Where is it?"

"Uh..." It took terrific effort to regain control, and with a trembling hand she pointed. "On the mantel." James gave a nod to Fellows who went to fetch it. Fearing that Fellows would start tossing more things about, she said, "It is in the silver frame."

He brought it back to James, who removed the picture from the frame and then handed it to him. "Put that back for me please." It was a copy of the photo that hung at the club.

"May we take this with us?"

"Oh, you are simply unbelievable. Yes, take whatever you like, I have no use for any of it anymore."

That statement rang like an alarm bell to say that he had taken it too far. She was as innocent as she claimed, and now he feared that she may have been so badly shaken that she might attempt to do herself harm. He didn't know it, but she was made of stronger stuff.

"Fellows, get on the telephone and have two agents sent over. I want to have two more here on guard twenty-four hours a day to watch over Miss Shaw until this is settled."

"Yes Sir." He went to the phone hanging on the wall in the kitchen.

"Watch over me? Am I under arrest now?"

"No," he said, softening his voice again in an effort to soothe her. "My suspicion of your involvement has been cleared away. I sincerely regret the way I have treated you, Miss Shaw, and I am sorry. However, there is the strong possibility that he intends to harm you. That is why I have asked my agents stay with you until this manhunt is over."

"You really think he might come here?"

"I do. Please understand, I cannot overstate the danger this man poses."

"Why?"

"Because you broke off your engagement, Miss Shaw. He is obviously an extremely vengeful man and has been killing people just for knowing him."

"Then I suppose that I have no choice."

"No, you don't. Forgive me please, for being so persistent, I have to be certain now that you are protected."

"I cannot forgive you, whoever you are," she said.

"I understand." James stood and waited until she would look at him.

"My name is Brigadier Horn; agent Fellows and I are with British Military Counterintelligence." He was about to leave, but a thought suddenly flashed through his mind. "You broke off the engagement, so you must have seen something undesirable in him."

"Yes, of course I did. He said something that made me see the wickedness in him."

"What did he say?"

"He accused his sister Jennifer of stealing his inheritance. He said that if there was a way of getting it back, even if he had to kill her to do it. That was unforgivable, and I told him so. I said, I could never love a man who could say such things. He turned on me, accusing me of taking his sister's side against him. He was being absolutely beastly and became more belligerent. I was left no choice but to end it with him."

"There it is. That was the act that has put you in jeopardy now. "

"Oh, God preserve me," she said, and stared down at the apron dusted in flour. "I suppose I should thank you now," she said, making eye contact with him again.

"It is not necessary."

"Good, then I won't."

James got to the door. "Wait," he said urgently. "You just told me that he threatened Jennifer."

"I did, why?"

"Oh, dear God, I have been such a fool! Fellows quickly, get on the telephone again we must warn the guards at Butterworth House that he may still be there. There's no time to lose!"

*****

CHAPTER ~ 13

THE KILLER GHOST

He had made his choice, it was simple enough at the time, but he had not given it enough thought to appreciate the fullness of the consequences of such a discussion.

It was in his nature to do everything that way, to act in the moment without due consideration. To seize each opportunity before it slipped away, that was the gambler in him. This time though, it had nothing to do with winning a

Dagg Hartogg aka,
Bart Butterworth

bet, or profit, of glory, or greed. It had meaning beyond anything that had gone before, it was choice of conscience, he thought.

Such was the result of the skill with which he had been conditioned to think. In spy parlance, he had been turned.

Following their capture at Tweebosch in February of 1902, something extraordinary had changed within Bart, a part at the very core of his being.

It forced him to open his eyes to Britain's rapacious and unscrupulous pursuit of Africa's treasures, its gold and diamonds. That was what started the war. He quickly changed sides and found safe haven across the Orange River.

Before the annexation of the Boer Republics to the British Empire in May of 1902, he and his ailing friend, Arthur Shaw made their way to the Netherlands where he became known as Dagg Hartogg, an employee in a furniture import export business. Soon after that he left Shaw in an Amsterdam hospital and moved to Germany settling in Hamburg for a while.

The moment he entered Germany they began his training in the department of propaganda. It was an impressive program of indoctrination aimed at switching over his patriotism and loyalty to Germany. During those sessions of re-education, Butterworth's ego was flying high, and he gave himself a rather over-the-top code name. He wanted to be known as the Ghost. His handler Lars Himmershold was willing to humour him, so he let it stick.

He was trained to be part of a group of insurgents in England, whose mission was to create havoc and destroy morale wherever they could. Again, feeding into his ego, his handler agreed to let him lead the operation.

Making regular visits from his room at Club 17 to his business in Amsterdam he established a solid cover for himself. And then the final part of his training was at hand. It had been planned from the moment Himmershold decided to use him in Johannesburg. So as to leave no doubt where his loyalties lay, Butterworth's first act of war was the murder of his dearest friend, Arthur Shaw.

In theory, Bart Butterworth was the perfect man to kill off to begin his campaign in earnest. He employed a devious plan to stage his demise and confuse the enemy. He purchased the plot where his victim would be laid to rest and ordered the gravestone.

Bartholomew Bigelow Butterworth Brother Betrothed Bastard.

His epitaph was an important part of the plan. If any of them bothered to visit his grave, they needed to see how he was wronged.

The ridiculous name that gave his so-called friends the ammunition for endless

Bart's Headstone

teasing. He was tormented by it his entire life. Brother of course, referred to his half sister who betrayed him and stole his inheritance. Betrothed referred to the beautiful woman who promised him love, and then broke that promise.

And finally, Bastard, the lie that he was the child born on the wrong side of the sheets. "No, not me, it was her. I am the rightful heir, and the Butterworth fortune should be mine." It was his way of showing everyone that all along, he knew what they had done to him. Yet his point might have been made clearer had he finished with a question mark.

And the brand, the arrows carved on the right edge of stone. Well, that was a joke of sorts. A small conceit, another expression of his displeasure. If they could understand it, they would see that it was the mark of a traitor and assume that he was the traitor.

But they would be wrong.

It was they who betrayed him, each and every one of them. And he was going to use that mark of betrayal as his signature for murder. If the police caught the significance of it, all to the good. But he thought they would be too dim to understand it. Surely, he thought, someone would come along who could explain it to them.

He took great care in laying out how each element was to be executed. His intention was to gradually make his victims suffer. One by one his so called friends, his mother, sister and fiancé, all those who had betrayed him, would pay for what they had done to him. His country as well, and he was going to see to it that the corrupt British Empire would fall before the might of Imperial Germany. There was nothing anyone could do to stop him now because you can't stop a ghost.

His choice of solicitor assured the most compliance with the least risk of betrayal.

His requirement of anonymity would ensure that the solicitor would never describe him to the authorities. He insisted that the solicitor send a letter to his half sister, which he dictated, informing her of his death, and asking her to come to London. She would see the stone and know that he was accusing her. Then he would bribe the solicitor's clerk, Mr. Stoat, to delay the posting of the letter for seventeen months. The date he chose was random, but as it happened, it would fit in nicely with the trend of world events. Then he set up his hapless friend for the disturbing suicide. Sgt. Fry was easy to bribe to be part of his plan. When the job was done, he was ready to go ahead.

Arthur's wound on the battlefield had destroyed most of the right side of his face and left him with permanent brain damage. Though the doctors managed to save his life, it was thought that he was little more than an empty vessel.

He could walk well enough, but in need of assistance to give him direction. It was amazing that James had described every detail of the murder so accurately. It was as if he had watched it happen.

Butterworth senior had offered Bart a building in central London, he owned several, and Bart selected 17 Catherine Place as it had everything he thought a gentlemen's club should have, plus one interesting feature that appealed to his childish sense of mischief. It had a network of secret passages that allowed access to almost every room in the house, as well as a secret entrance at the back. He chose not to share the existence of those amusing architectural features with anyone.

After dark, one day in January 1913, he used that entrance to usher Arthur inside. He sat him in the wing chair in the Collections Room, spread newspaper on the floor and then shot him, attempting to destroy the scars of his original wound. With Fry there to 'discover' the body and identify it as Bartholomew Butterworth his plan began perfectly. Now as the ghost, he was free do whatever he liked. God save the Kaiser.

Later Bartholomew, the ghost, brought in twenty-eight agents and set up a base of operations in Belfast. He paired off the majority into ten two-man teams to carry out the work of sabotage and information gathering.

The rest were navy men, sailors whose task was to crew the ship that ferried the agents back and forth across the Irish Sea to England over the next year. They moved ashore and blended into the countryside as much as possible while they waited for the agents to complete their assignments.

His plan was working perfectly, until James Horn happened along.

*****

REVENGE TRUMPS EVERYTHING

It was early in that July of 1914, just before the war began. On Himmershold's orders, Dagg Hartogg sailed from Amsterdam to Belfast to select his crew for the mission. On the *Kingfisher* they voyaged from Belfast south to Wales and a berth at a wharf in Cardiff Bay.

The *Kingfisher*

He moved inland with his team, Jacob Yost and Velma Holesing, who were specially trained to provoke fear and panic within the civilian population. They travelled to London by train and established a safe house in Whitechapel where he left them to do their work.

Picking their targets in communities along the Thames they began spreading rumours of government plots against the Irish and Irish plots of revenge. Then, planting bombs at a post office and a marketplace they killed dozens of people and injured more. And while the smoke settled, they wormed their way into the crowds pointing the blame for their acts of terrorism at the Irish separatists and the Suffragette movement.

Those of Irish decent became targets of revenge and the police treated the suffragettes more cruelly than before.

Through the lens of his new-found allegiance, he could see that all the problems of his life were laid upon him and clearly not of his doing. It was clear to him that he was owed a great deal for the suffering he had endured, and he would begin collecting that debt now. While his agents revelled in patriotic terrorism, he settled into his personal agenda, and the first on his list was Jennifer.

Bart waited for his half sister to turn up from Switzerland. Her notice in the personal column announced her arrival. After that, it wasn't terribly difficult to follow her about and see what she would make of his game.

He expected her to visit the solicitor which she did, but for some unfathomable reason she didn't enter the building. She went back several times and each time she paused before deciding to leave. The last time she went it was a grey and chilly day with the promise of rain. He was unhappy to be standing out on the street, shivering, and wishing she would just follow through with it at last. But just as before she hesitated.

"Damn," he cursed, tossing his cigarette to the pavement and grinding it down with his toe. He was ready to hail a cab to follow her back to her hotel when she did the unexpected.

When she left this time, she had her driver follow a man who had just come out of the office building. "What the hell is she doing now?"

He stopped a cab and pointed out her car to his driver then told him to follow it. It was easy enough to do, as the man his sister was following had chosen to ride in a Hansom Cab.

When the Hansom stopped on Warwick Square, Jennifer's car pulled up at the corner to let her out.

Bart had his cab turn around and drop him on the opposite side of the road.

Her pursuit of that man puzzled Bart. What did she want with him? She seemed to know him, yet the stranger had not a clue who she was.

After a brief conversation at his door, his demeanour changed from irritation to welcoming and he invited her in. What had she said to him? What was he to her? Why had she followed him in the first place?

Bart crossed the street and walked by the house they had entered and saw the plaque by the door. Messrs Horn and Hillman Private Investigators. Uh-ha, she had sought out professional help. That could be a problem, he thought, and having no idea how long she would spend in that house, he had to work quickly.

There was a phone box back at the corner. Rushing to it he called the safe house to order the man he brought with him to London to hurry over and watch the place. Yost arrived a half hour later and took over the surveillance.

He hopped the fence of the small Warwick Square Park, found a spot in the bushes and settled in for an uncomfortable reconnaissance in the rain.

There was no report from Yost by the end of the day and Bart realised that having a subordinate do the job for him was a mistake. Something was amiss and he wasn't able to find out what had happened. He never heard from the man again. Worse still, Jennifer had vanished. He went to her hotel and found that she had moved out without leaving a forwarding address.

The opportunity was lost, and with that part of his plan ruined, reluctantly, he was forced to move on and finish his scheme.

The remaining members of the Enlightened Twelve were next. Those little minded pigs who had suckled at his teat for so long, they owed him, and it was time to pay up.

Butterworth had been hiding in the secret passageways for days, obsessed with listening to everything that was going on. He told himself that he was waiting for the right time to strike. Actually, the narcissist was waiting for them to talk about him but, apparently, they had forgotten all about him and it was driving him mad.

Then he heard that two men would be coming in to seek a place on the membership roll. Timothy Blackwood was to lunch with them and show them around. Well Timmy old chum, you'll be the first to go.

Hard luck had followed Bart since he arrived in London, and it just seemed to continue until this moment. He recognized the name of one of the men as the same fellow Jennifer had followed from the solicitor's office. If her detectives were coming in, then something was cooking on Jennifer's fire.

They arrived as scheduled and were greeted by Sgt. Fry like old friends. That too was as unwelcome as it was unexpected.

As he listened to their conversation he learned that the detectives were there not to talk about their membership, but his suicide. Clearly, they had seen through his attempt to make it look like suicide.

He had made several mistakes that those men must have picked up on right away and they were convinced that it was murder.

They had slashed through his pride as a sabre would through a body and for a moment left him feeling utterly defeated. But as he continued to listen

His pride was somewhat restored. They confessed that even after finding all his silly clues they were still unable to decipher their meaning. Without understanding their meaning, they would never question the identity of the corpse, and his plan could continue.

He was about to leave and try again later, but then Will Jenkins barged in and their conversation ended, giving rise to a new conversation. Jenkins had heard a bit of what they were saying and hurried in to remind Tim of their pact to never mention Bart's name again.

So that was it. That was why he had spent so many days waiting for someone to mention him without joy. It was because they couldn't forget him. That was even better. He gave them the club, he led then as a team of officers in South Africa, and now the mere mention of his name had some power over them. He was a ghost haunting them effortlessly, unintentionally by proxy. They couldn't cut him out of their history. Soon they would actually face the ghost and he would cut them from his.

He had to act quickly.

Following the two so-called friends upstairs, he knew that the others would be going out to lunch, while Tim had to stay because of his guests downstairs. He would be alone for a moment. It was perfect.

He waited for the others to head off, then came out of the room across the hall just as Blackwood appeared from the card room. "I say, Tim. Hello, just the man I was looking for."

"Yes?" he said, turning and then he froze. "Bart?! But you're dead!"

With gun in hand Butterworth grinned, "I'm a ghost, up from Hell, Timmy boy, to take you back with me."

"What...?"

"Just shut up and move," pointing to the Men's Lounge he said, "in there. There's some little thing I need to take care of."

The rest was pure invention.

"And what would that be?" asked Tim.

"You, dear boy." As soon as the door closed behind them, he smacked Blackwood on the head with his revolver. Ripping the pull cord from the curtains he strangled Timothy to death. Then using his pen knife, he gleefully cut the two arrows symbol into his wrist.

As Tim was a lean young man, it wasn't difficult to lift him into position facing the wall and hold him there while he lynched him on the lighting fixture. Lastly, Butterworth quietly tipped over the chair, then disappeared into his hole in the wall like a rat.

Down on the main floor he appeared again, this time at the back of the tiny office that Sergeant Flynn occupied. "Here, what the... My God, it's you! What are you doing here?"

"Just popped in to see an old friend off. As a matter of fact, I have another job for you, Archie." He told him to go upstairs and discover his second suicide victim. Completely unnerved, the old man ran off to do his bidding without a thought to what might happen after he did his part.

Once again Butterworth hid in the passageway to wait until the police had finished up their useless investigation.

It would be an interesting exercise to have the private detectives step in and do a thorough poke about before the police arrived. Would they be able to find a flaw in this murder?

Fry hadn't had any warning that there would be other killings and he was terrified that he would be found out, tried and hanged as an accomplice.

When James asked to talk with him in the Collections Room, he knew he was done and be forced to confess his part in the first cover-up. He panicked and made a run for it.

When Bart heard the commotion as James and Anthony gave chase, he snatched Flynn from the back staircase and broke his neck. He flung the old man down the steps in the secret passageway and the noise of it alerted the detectives to where he was.

They had already discovered his hidden door and chased after Fry all the way down to the cellar. It was all Bart could do to get out of the house before they found his body.

The police wouldn't be fooled like that again. If there was any good to be found in this precarious situation, they would never know that their murder was a ghost. The club was off limits now, but his campaign was far from over. Now that he knew who the new participants were he immediately began devising his next murder. And this time, he would do it with an audience.

Immediately after eliminating Will Jenkins, Bart took the train down to Cardiff and returned to the Kingfisher ordering his crew to set sail for Belfast. Before they arrived, he got a radio message from one of his agents that his half sister had returned to Butterworth House. That news spawned an idea of how he might deal with the three most important debtors, the women who ruined his life.

*****

CHAPTER ~ 14

HOSTAGES AT BUTTERWORTH HOUSE

The Army vehicle sped through the city with a siren blaring, and causing all obstacles to scatter or risk being crushed. James held on for dear life as the car skidded over the cobble stones and leaped over the curbs as it took the curves. Other vehicles joined the race to Butterworth House.

When they reached the forest trail James silenced the siren, but Fellows maintained the pace all the way to the gate of the mansion.

The first man they found lay dead in the grass. His throat had been cut, his body still warm and the blood fresh, telling them that the killer had only arrived a short time ago, and made his approach silently. The second man had been shot dead at the door, his rifle still slung over his shoulder. The door was locked, and the moment Fellows tried the latch a bullet fired from inside, ripped through the wood and killed the agent instantly.

"Hold your fire!" James shouted.

"Hello! I know that voice," said Butterworth, from the other side and sounding pleased with himself.

"It's that nuisance private detective, Horn, isn't it? Tell me Horn, did I just kill your partner?"

"No, but you ended the life of another fine young man. And I recognise your voice as well. We spoke on the telephone, you claiming to be Will Jenkins. Were you hoping to kill me as well, or were you just looking for an audience to see you murder a man in cold blood?"

"Oh, very good deduction there. Yes, I did want you there as my audience for that one."

"And you killed the policeman near the park."

"Yes, he was very useful."

"You wrote to Jennifer claiming to be a friend. Did you bring her here simply to be a witness to your madness, or did you lure her to London to be slaughtered like the rest?"

"My goodness, you seem to know a great deal. But I'm willing to bet that is all you know."

"Then you would lose that bet. I know a great deal more. You are going by the name of Dagg Hartogg, recruited by the Germans following your capture in South Africa and now you spy for them. You wanted us to believe that you were Arthur Shaw and that Arthur murdered you at the club, but your staging was poorly thought out and clumsily executed."

"Are you just trying to anger me?"

"No, I am simply pointing out your many shortcomings, Butterworth. You are a traitor to the British Empire, and a coward hiding behind the murder of your best friend." There was a long silence from inside, during which James quietly gave orders to find a way inside. With that set as the priority, he went back to his plan to give his people enough time to do their job. "Bart, are you still there?"

"I am." He paused. "I suppose you think you deserve congratulations for the fine detective work." His bravado had waned, and he was sounding more like a petulant child.

"Oh please," James shot back. "Don't flatter yourself. It was hardly a challenge to find where the blame lies. But before we explore that in depth, I need to know who you have in there with you."

"You want a count of my confederates?"

"That would be useful of course, but I was actually referring to your hostages. Are your sister and stepmother there with you?"

"Oh, you mean the parasite bitch that laid her egg in my nest… her, and the bloody cowbird hatchling that booted me out of it?"

"If you say so, very poetic and all that, but my question is are they there?"

"Yes, why not? They are both here."

"And are they both alive?"

"For now… But as you might imagine, it's just a matter of time before I rectify that problem."

"Use your head man, at the moment, their safety is the only thing I care about."

"Is it? Well, frankly, how sad is that? They deserve to die for what they did to me."

"Surely you don't really believe that do you?"

"I certainly do."

By this time agents from MI-2H had surrounded the house and scanned the windows for other hostiles inside. One man reported seeing a woman with a candle in a third-floor window. But now one had found a way in. That message was delivered to James with a shrug and a shake of the head. James was beginning to think this was hopeless.

Barging in would certainly result in Butterworth and his accomplices killing their hostages. The only option he could see was giving the man what he wanted. "Listen to me."

"I'm listening," said Butterworth. His responses were weak, the authority with which he had handled the earlier conversation was gone. James wondered if that was in his favour, or had he once again, gone too far?

"Alright, that's a good start. I'm prepared to negotiate with you for their release, and for the release of the staff. They are all alive I hope."

"If hopes were horses... Oh, Horn, did you see what I did there? Another poem." James held his tongue. "Anyway, we lost old Fish, I'm afraid. He's dead."

"You are talking about Mr. Perch I assume."

"I never liked the old bugger, couldn't understand a thing he said. Did you know that he tried to lock me out of my own house?"

"No, I didn't know that."

"That got him a bullet in the head for his pains. Josi will survive, I suppose. Unless you do something stupid."

"I said we could negotiate their release. My first condition is that you ..."

"So, you believe that you are in a position to dictate terms? No sir, that's not the way this is going to work. I make the rules and you do as I say." He was reviving his authority now and James thought that perhaps it would be safer to let him go on thinking he was in control.

"Alright, let's talk about it. How do you propose we do this?"

"You are missing the point, old man. There will be no discussion. You do as I say, or I will set off the explosives and reduce this house to rubble."

"Then we would all die."

"So you see my point."

"Please, don't do that. I could arrange for some sort of reduced sentence. I could take the firing squad off the table."

"There, you see where I have a problem with your form of negotiation? I know what awaits me if I give myself up to you."

"How could you? There are ways that we could…"

"Horn, give it up. That doesn't work for me at all. No, I want free passage out of Scotland and guarantees that you won't be coming after me."

"And if I agree to that, you will let them all go?"

"Why not?" he said, as if that sounded like a fine idea.

"Do I have your oath that you will abide by your part of our agreement?"

He snorted with laughter. "Of course, you do."

"Will you give me something to demonstrate your good will?"

"Possibly. I can be gracious, what do you want?"

Henrietta was the person he wanted first. "I understand that your stepmother is unwell. Will you release her to me so that she can receive medical attention?"

"No, she's fine where she is, thank you very much. I'll tell you what I will do, however. I'll send out Josi, how does that sound?"

"Alright, I'll accept that. Send her out now."

"Oh no. I'll need something from you first. You have the house surrounded. I want them all gone before I let her out."

"Alright, I can arrange that. I'll need some time to evacuate everyone."

Henrietta Butterworth,
Actress Henrietta
as Lady Macbeth

"How much time should I give you?"

"An hour, give me an hour."

"Not good enough. It took perhaps five minutes for them to surround the house. So, that is all the time you get to remove them before I start killing people. And the clock starts now."

"You can't be serious!" James turned to his people and shouted frantically, "Alright, everyone except for my driver, pull back and leave the area immediately. Return to Glasgow HQ." Calling to the man closest to him, "You there, spread the word and be quick about it!"

"Sir!"

"Bravo detective. They really hop to it when you speak, don't they? I'm guessing that makes you something more than a private detective now doesn't it.

"I am simply a soldier in the British Army."

"Of course, you are. You mentioned a driver. Where is he now?"

"At the automobile I suppose, I don't know, to be honest. You shot the man who brought me here."

"Oh yes, the man you said was not your partner. I do hope you weren't lying about that. It seemed like such a lovely friendship you two gentlemen have. I would hate to be the one who spoiled it."

With perhaps a minute to spare, all the agents had left the property. "Bart, I've done my bit, now you do yours."

Butterworth didn't answer and the silence stretched on.

"Hello, Bartholomew, my agents are gone, send out Josi now."

Several minutes staggered by with not a word from inside and James had a sick feeling as he approached the door. "Butterworth," he shouted, as he banged on the heavy wooden slab. "Butterworth!"

The lock turned with a clunk, the latch moved and the door opened slowly. "Don't shoot," said the frightened little voice, "It only me, Josi."

James barged in and did a quick scan of the hallway and the rooms on each side as he ran to the stairs.

"They've all gone, sir. While you was waitin' out there, they used the underground passage to the wee path by river. I saw him take the ladies to a car parked down there and drive off across the bridge."

"What?"

"Aye, sir. Mr. Hollister B had secret passages build all over the place."

"Damn, damn him to hell!" He ran to the window at the back of the house and saw them disappear off into the distance. "Damn! How is it that my people didn't find it?"

"You wouldn't know it was there, sir, unless you was walking by the shore."

Bart's bridge to freedom across the White Cart Water.

*****

CHAPTER ~ 15

CHASING THE GHOST

Every mile seemed endless, every bump on the road a painful reminder that he had miscalculated, missed a major clue. The result could mean the man would get away, free to kill again, free to continue bringing his brand of warfare back home to England. It could already be too late for his hostages. With his successful escape from Butterworth House there was no reason that he could see, for Butterworth to keep them alive. That in itself was a tragedy, another failure. But he knew that Miss Shaw would be safe for now, protected as she was in her little house with the blue door.

What kept him going was the chance that Butterworth might be heading back to his ship which had been beached at Cardwell Bay, near Gourock. Anthony had arrived in Glasgow during the standoff at Butterworth House. When the agents returned as ordered and told him what had gone on there, he anticipated what James might have done in order to save the women and organized a squad of men to back him up.

Feeling certain that Butterworth would be heading to Gourock to make his escape, he too set off for the tiny coastal village.

But in case he was late getting there, he alerted the navy that he might be too late and that they should send out a patrol from Greenock. The Navy was eager to get in on the action and sent out two Kil-class patrol guns the *Kilberry* and the *Kilbeggan*, to scour the area.

*****

THE ENEMY ON THE BEACH

When the tide lifted the *Kingfisher* off the beach they moved out to deeper water and anchored.

While he left a good ten minutes before James, he was forced to cross the bridge to escape, and that road took him south into Pollok. From there his trek would be a long slow winding lane all the way to Gourock.

James went the only way he knew, heading north to the river and then west to Gourock. His driver, a local man, was able to make good time and passed through Port Glasgow just a couple of minutes after Butterworth.

Anthony had headed their way in a lorry with ten soldiers and three of his agents who had travelled with him from London. They were moving a little slower as they had to make their way through the busy streets of Glasgow and were further delayed at the drawbridge over White Cart Water. As they drove through Inchinnan, they were passed by a vehicle carrying two women. One appeared to be slumped down in the back seat, but it was moving so quickly that Anthony couldn't get a good look from the passenger seat.

"Wiggins, did you see that woman in the back seat?"

Velma kidnaps Cynthia Shaw

"Yes, that's what I thought too, but I wasn't sure. Thank you." Anthony closed his eyes as he agonized over the decision he was about to make. If he followed that car there was a chance, probably a good one, that it wasn't going to Cardwell Bay and he'd be no help to James. But he had a terrible feeling that the woman bound had something to do with what James doing. Following it may be the best choice. "Alright, follow them wherever they go. Try to keep up with them but not too close."

"Yes Sir."

*****

FROM HAMILTON DRIVE

Velma Holesing had made her way to Cynthia Shaw's house wearing a suffragette sash over her plain white dress and a broad brimmed white hat that had become a uniform for the movement. As instructed, she was driving a fast car she'd stolen in Edinburgh the previous day.

As she walked to the house she straightened the sash and adjusted the hat carefully as any woman of quality would. Cynthia saw her coming from the window and went to the door to greet her.

"Good afternoon, Miss Shaw. We are having a rally at the Union Hall and I was sent down to pick you up."

"Gracious me, I knew nothing about a meeting."

"Oh, a very last minute thing, you know how it is. Please, you must hurry and get changed or we will be late."

Velma's accent was good but not perfect and Cynthia picked it up right away. "Of course. I didn't catch your name."

"Rose Parker, don't you remember? We met at the Scottish Council for Women's Trades on Renfield Street."

"Oh yes, of course we did. Alright, well I won't be long then. Just wait here while I change." With that Cynthia headed for the back door through the kitchen.

"I thought I had overplayed my part," Velma said, aiming her Luger at Cynthia's back. Cynthia turned slowly and backed away, coming to rest against the kitchen counter. It was amazing, she thought, how quickly she had become used to having a gun pointed at her. "What gave me away?"

"Actually, there were so many things, it is difficult to know where to begin," she said, making it sound as insulting as possible. "What do you want?"

"What do I want? Nothing. It is your fiancé who wants you. Now hurry upstairs and change. He specifically wanted to see you in that white dress."

"I won't do it."

Velma raised the gun aiming it at Cynthia's head. "Then I will kill you here, it is all the same to me. Is that how it will be?"

"Very well, I'll change. Wait here."

"We have already tried it your way. Now we do it my way. Go ahead, I will be right behind you." The moment Cynthia had dressed in her Suffrage uniform Velma stepped up behind her and clubbed her on the head with her gun. Cynthia dropped like a stone. Demonstrating her strength, Velma carried her victim down the stairs and out to the car. Her destination was the beach at Cardwell Bay, and she was in a desperate hurry before Kingfisher set sail without her.

She passed a military transport so quickly she nearly lost control and it frightened her. Not giving the lorry a second thought, she raced on. All she cared about now was the road ahead and staying on it. It never occurred to her to look back in the rear-view mirror. Had she done so, she would have seen the lorry was now following her at a discreet distance.

*****

First to Arrive

Wheeling into Greenock like a man possessed, Butterworth streaked through town, and passed Fort Matilda at 60 miles per hour. His recklessness drew little attention from the troops inside training to head to the front. Their training was being supplied, for the most part, by Boer War veterans, men too old or medically unfit for service at the front.

Men who knew the face of war were not easily distracted by the silliness of civilians as they took pains to prepare their students for what was to come.

His passengers, now dressed in white, were being watched by Carl Speirs, the agent who had joined Butterworth to replace the man killed in London. A small man, Speirs, had a disquieting way of smiling all the time, as if he knew what was going to happen to them and it thrilled him.

"Do you really need to wave that thing at us? We have no way of escaping."

"Does it frighten you, this pistol? It is an excellent killing machine. The 1904 Imperial Navy Luger."

"I suppose threatening us with it makes you feel more like a man. But you're still just a boy, aren't you?"

"You should not say such things to me!"

"Carl, shut up."

He ignored Butterworth and continued to stare at them, and the intensity in his blue eyes suggested the depraved thoughts that boiled behind them. "I am very much going to enjoy killing you."

Jennifer was putting on a brave face for the benefit of her mother, but she was terrified.

Her brother had repeatedly told them that they were going for a sea voyage and would never reach port alive. But Carl Speirs' version of the future seemed quite different. Coinciding with his boast they arrived at the stone covered beach and Bart parked at the edge.

The crew had left the lifeboat behind so that Bart could row out to them.

But seeing that the small ship swing at anchor with its sail being hoisted to half mast, Bart mistakenly thought that he was being left behind. Both angry and terrified he was ready to snap and needed to do something to relieve the pressure and Carl had just given him the perfect release.

"Carl," Bart said, as he got out of the car, "I warned you, yet you chose to ignore me, so this is where we part company."

And as if to punctuate his reprimand he raised his own Luger and shot the young man in the head.

Both women screamed as Carl tipped over and fell to the ground.

"Shut up!" Bart yelled and they shrank back in fear of what he might do next. "Alright. Get out and start walking to the little boat."

"Do you really mean to kill us Bart?"

"After the way you both treated me so dishonestly, is that so surprising?"

"Bart," Jennifer said, "we never treated you unfairly. I offered you half the company after father died and you refused it."

"It should have been mine, all of it! I was the rightful heir, not the bastard."

"Bart! How dare you speak to your sister like that?"

"Oh, do be quiet Henrietta. You gold digging whore, you're no better than she. If I'm not mistaken, you helped dear old Daddy murder my mother, so your head is definitely on the chopping block," and pushed them away from the car.

Making their way over the slippery stones and shells was difficult in the shoes they wore, and Jennifer had to hold Henrietta's hand to keep her steady and upright. As they drew near the small craft, the further away the Kingfisher seemed and Bart's whole body felt like it was trembling.

Then he heard the sound of James' military sedan roaring up and screeching to a stop. All three of them turned to see who had come. The women with rising hopes of rescue, and Bart feeling the utter despair of failure.

The driver pulled up by Carl Speirs's body and James leaped out with his gun drawn, shouting. "That's far enough Butterworth. Not a step further!"

Grasping his Lee-Enfield 303, the driver jumped out, fed a bullet into the breach and took his stance levelling his rifle at the enemy.

Self-preservation moved Bart as he quickly skirted around the women to put them between himself and the guns.

The showdown on the beach

Frustrated, James shouted, "Give it up man. There is no escape for you now."

"No? You won't mind if I disagree, will you, old man?" He pulled a sword from his side and raised it up to unsheathe it with unnecessary dramatics.

Quietly, James spoke to his driver. "Hold your fire," then to Butterworth, "Be reasonable man, we have been through this before. There are no tricks left to deceive each other, the choice is simple. You give it up and release the hostages or you die here."

"Then I suppose that I shall die here," he said, tossing the sheath aside.

"But what will that accomplish? There is no great victory for your new masters to be had here. All you will have accomplished is ugly, pointless murder."

"Oh, I should say there has been purpose. I will have destroyed the people who made my life a living hell."

"I'm afraid that you only have one person to blame for that, Butterworth. You have done that yourself."

"No," he shouted. "These women are the ones who have done it to me. They..."

His rant was interrupted as another automobile could be heard in the near distance. They all turned to look and in that instant of distraction Butterworth ran his stepmother through with his sword.

She gasped with pain and Jennifer screamed as both women looked down at his hand pushing the blade through to its hilt. The blade, dripping with her blood protruded from her back.

"Oh God!" Jennifer screamed. "Mother!" A red stain began to spread down her dress and as he began to draw it out Henrietta dropped to her knees. Still holding her hand, Jennifer shouted at him, "How could you be so beastly?"

"Obviously, with no particular difficulty whatsoever, my dear."

She growled back "There is no doubt who the bastard is now!"

"No? I think I'll take your head now."

Another scream rang out from second motorcar. It was Cynthia's cry for help this time. Reacting instinctively, the soldier swung his rifle around just in time to see the driver point her weapon at her hostage in the back.

The showdown on the beach

Without hesitation, he fired killing Velma. That shot drew Butterworth's attention away just as he raised his sword to strike at Jennifer's neck. James seized his chance to take the shot. It brought the mad man down with a bullet to the face.

James ran down the beach and knelt beside Henrietta. "She's bleeding terribly," Jennifer said. "I don't know what to do." "Here," James said, as he pulled out his pocketknife and ripped the hem of Henrietta's dress to make a compress. "Jennifer, hold this against the wound both front and back, and apply pressure."

The Germans opened fire from the deck of *Kingfisher*, but their shots were falling short. "It won't take long before they get their range," he said. "Have you got this?"

"Yes, I think so. Thank you."

"Alright, we have to move her, keep the pressure on. He lifted the woman up and with Jennifer keeping pace they headed to the roadway and some protection.

While James was gathering Henrietta up in his arms, Anthony and his troops arrived. Immediately the men bailed out of the lorry, formed a firing line and began letting off volley after volley of covering fire.

Terrified, Jennifer huddled close to James as they made their way to the only shelter there was for them, behind the car holding Cynthia.

The thin metal of the coachwork offered little against the high-powered Mauser M1887, the same weapons that James had faced in South Africa. Laying Henrietta on the ground, he said, "Keep pressure on it." He opened the door of the vehicle and cut the ropes that bound Cynthia then helped her down to sit beside Jennifer and her mother.

"Anthony! How wonderful of you to show up! I couldn't be more pleased to see you."

"Always a pleasure, James," his friend answered, from fifty feet away.

"Can you shift the lorry over here to shield the women from those rifles?"

"Right. Driver, you heard the brigadier, hop to it then."

"Yes Sir." He cranked up the engine again and then swung it in front of the motorcar. The lorry provided little real protection from the high powered rifles the German sailors were using, but they felt safer behind it.

Marksmen crouched behind the gunwale were choosing their targets carefully and as their shots came closer bits of metal and wood began to rain down on James and the women.

The Kingfisher's captain spotted it long before the men on shore did. He realised that he would never outrun the HMS *Kilbeggan* but at least he was going try. He ordered his crew to prepare to make way as soon as the anchor cleared the river bottom.

The ship slipped with the current as the gaff was hoisted to the top of the mast and when the mainsail began to catch the wind the captain steered her to the open sea. Only then did the rate of fire slack off.

That was the moment those ashore saw the black smoke appear against the hills on the far side of the river. A roaring cheer went up from the soldiers.

James felt some relief when a medic arrived at his side to attend Henrietta. Moments after that, soldiers carried her on a litter to his vehicle and rushed to the military base hospital.

"It's hard to say for certain, Sir, but I don't think the sword pierced anything vital, so she may be alright."

"Thank you, corpsman. You'll stay with her until she is seen by a doctor?"

"Yes Sir, I will." Without further delay she was driven way from the beach.

As far as James was concerned the case was over and he was much relieved. All that remained was to dispatch the *Kingfisher* and its crew.

*****

Battle at Sea

The HMS *Kilbeggan* steamed into view and soon this battle would be over.

The gunboat's lookout had no trouble spotting the battle between the fishing boat and the beach and identified the vessel as the one Brigadier Horn had described.

"Can you make out the men on shore?"

"Aye, they're our boys, Captain."

"Very well. Forward gunner put a shot across the bow of that ship."

"Aye Sir."

"Fire when ready."

With a great boom the shell went streaking across the Clyde and sent up a large plume of water ahead of the small Dutch ship. It seemed to have no effect of the people on its deck. The gun battle continued.

"Forward Gunner."

"Aye Captain."

Kil-class patrol gunboat *HMS Kilbeggan*

For a second time a lick of flame and smoke erupted from Let's see if we can put bloody *Kingfisher* out of action."

"Firing on *Kingfisher*, aye, aye Captain."

For a second time a lick of flame and smoke erupted from the gun and a shell ripped through the air with a terrible scream, striking the wooden vessel amidships, just above the waterline, and exploded. With a mighty wallop the enemy boat was obliterated.

Down the shoreline at Fort Matilda, the soldiers in training were allowed to break off to watch *Kilbeggan* steam up the river and when it fired its gun, demolishing the fishing boat, hundreds of voices could be heard in loud sustained cheering.

"Target destroyed, Captain."

"Very well. Well done lads. Helmsman…"

"Aye Captain?"

"Reduce speed to ten knots and turn us about. Our job is done here, make way back to port at three quarter speed."

"Aye, aye Captain. Engine room, coming about, reduce speed to ten knots."

"Signalman," said the captain as he took his seat, "hail HMS *Kilberry* and inform her captain that the vessel *Kingfisher* has been located, engaged, and destroyed, *Kilbeggan* returning to port. Regards, Duncan MacIntyre."

"Aye, aye Sir."

"He'll be so put out you'll be able to fry an egg on his bald head." The crew in the wheelhouse had a good laugh over that one. The young captain was well liked by his crew. He was tough and drilled them until they could do their jobs in their sleep, but he was fair, and had a quiet sense of humour.

*****

EPILOGUE

THE BATTLE IS OVER

It is hard to view any part of this case as being lucky though, for those who survived, luck certainly played a part. Henrietta Butterworth survived, as her luck was due to the careless placement of her stepson's sword. It missed everything of importance internally and though it would take time for her to heal and recover from the ordeal, recover she would. To be sure, Cynthia was concussed and suffered headaches for some time to come, she too survived.

Jennifer continued to run her shipping company from Glasgow, committing many of her freighters to the use of the Royal Navy. Butterworth suffered some losses while carrying troops and supplies across the Atlantic from America and Canada. But under Jennifer's stewardship, Butterworth Shipping invested heavily in the shipbuilding yards at Greenock and Port Glasgow along the Clyde.

Though it was a small victory, for its first time out MI-2$_H$ proved itself by eliminating the Bartholomew Bigelow Butterworth cell. Some of his German agents who were not involved in the skirmish on the beach remained active for many months.

There would be many more investigations as the counter-intelligence department of MI-2$_H$ moved to uncover Germany's plans to wreak havoc on the cities and towns of England.

Quickly promoted to Major General James Wilson Horn, 3rd Earl of Reedmont, led MI-2$_H$ from London, while Brigadier Hillman ran the school. James' indomitable curiosity and Anthony's skill, wit and imagination would serve them both well throughout the war.

****

THE END

THE WAR CONTINUED

About the Author

Hugh Russel

Hugh Russel lives with his wife Cheryl in the township of Mulmur, north of Toronto.

Trained as a commercial artist, he began his career painting and illustrating. He moved into radio to supplement his income, or more accurately to actually have an income. He was a broadcaster for eleven years telling stories about family life and living in Toronto. In his mid-thirties, he turned his attention to sculpting, creating works in bronze, terra cotta, and wood which have been included in collections all over the world, notably the Column of Brotherhood now situated in Vatican City. He has been telling and writing stories forever but only recently has he begun to fine tune those stories for publication. Hugh says he has had more fun writing these stories than anything else he has ever done and the best part he says, is you can just make stuff up.

*****

Other books by Hugh Russel

Book 1, Kat in Harm's Way

Book 2, To Kill Kat

Hugh Russel